Brothers
of
Survival

Cal Davis

DEDICATION

For Lydia, Attikus, Lillian, and Adonis

Reading should be fun!

Table of Contents

A Note to the Reader: This is a tale of survival, resilience, and healing. As part of the character's journey, the story addresses difficult topics, including allusions to physical abuse. These themes are handled with sensitivity and are not depicted in graphic detail. Please be mindful of this content as you read.

Section 1

Keyloi gazed up the slope to where his house should have been, but he found only a raw, naked landscape. The few trees that remained standing around him seemed like lonely survivors, others farther on having been utterly erased, leaving nothing but barren earth.

A wound had been carved into the world. Where a city once stood, now a void. No buildings, no streets, just a breathtaking emptiness that stretched from the mountain to the sea. The closer he walked, the more complete the destruction became, until he was forced to stop, his mind reeling from the sheer scale of it. He had never imagined devastation of this magnitude; a sight so absolute that his brain refused to process it. He could only stand and stare, trapped in a moment of pure, uncomprehending horror.

***

Sabao knocked on the entrance at Keyloi's house. Soon the two were on the floor playing a game they had learned at school that day. Keyloi and his best friend, Sabao, were inseparable. As iconic members of the Hustaka Elite team, they practiced their routines regularly and developed new jumps and hurls. As highly intelligent and agile young males, the two excelled with an innate agility in hustaka, an extreme form of acrobatics.

"We're going to kill the Ramblers in the game this week. That will put us in place to go to the Hemisphere of Hustaka event," Keyloi was jubilant about the game.

"Yes, if you can do your double twist right this time," Sabao ribbed.

"Wait a second. I did it better than you did your split hurl." The boys laughed.

Born to Relacin and Motatia Kontes, Keyloi had a rosy complexion and sparkling green eyes which were typical of Radzierians. His medical doctor father and Level 12 instructor mother always ensured he would gain as much knowledge and exposure to life as could be provided and encouraged him to get involved with neighborhood and civic activities.

Radzierian space exploration began two centuries earlier, and the planet was one of the six-member planets of the Intergalactic Alliance. Dr. Kontes was a pivotal part of research and development for the Alliance. Radzierian intuitive abilities were exceptional, and the Alliance benefited from that ability for humanoid interrelations.

Mom called them for a quick lunch. "We need to get moving so we won't be late for practice." The friends were never late and usually pushed the adults to arrive sooner.

"You know you twisted wrong on that last move. That's why Pracia fell," Keyloi teased.

Sabao snickered as he moved his crimson hair from his eyes. "It was funny, but the instructor didn't think so. And she didn't get hurt."

"I don't know about that," Keyloi chuckled. "She looked like this." He waved his arms from side to side and bobbed his head.

"You look like a Pulodian." Laughter followed.

"Careful, boys," Mom chided the pair. "You know Pulodians are intelligent creatures, and we should never tease others. They are just a different species."

"Yes, Tani." The boys responded in unison, gaining their composure.

Sabao, always the curious one, asked, "Tani, why don't we ever see them?"

Mom thought for a few seconds. "We will someday. They just stay on their side of the planet for now, and we stay on ours. I guess it's best that way." She didn't look convinced of her own explanation.

Keyloi's mother's instruction at the city school focused on social and cultural relations.

"Can we go visit them?" Always full of adventure, Keyloi raised his eyes.

"Uh, not today." His mother busied herself by putting the

meal together. "Maybe someday when relations are more established." She looked up at the boys and said, "You two need to get ready to go. You have practice soon."

"Yes, Tani." The young males answered simultaneously and changed into their hustaka wear.

"Tani Motatia, why don't we have communication with the Pulodians? There are Radzierians in the Intergalactic Alliance who travel all over the multiverse to find life and build relations, but we don't know much about these creatures on our own planet."

Mom smiled. "Sabao, you are always seeking answers. That's a good trait."

"Thank you, Tani," he lowered his head.

"Pulodians were never really understood by Radzierians. They have lived in the southern hemisphere with a cooler climate for thousands of years. It was only until the last one hundred years that they were noted to have progressed enough for us to know that they are more than just flora or fauna. They are not humanoids, but they have intelligence and reasoning as humanoids do. They do not have vocal cords, so they cannot speak humanoid languages, and there are no translations of their language. They have their own dwellings, culture, civilization, educational system, but no humanoid has been able to fully assimilate with them. We have shared our techniques with them, and we have adopted some of their methods as well. Maybe someday someone will get an accurate translation system for them, and we will learn about an entirely new race of intelligent, non-humanoid creatures. You will learn much more about them in Level 9." Teacher Mom had surfaced at home again.

"But that's two years away. I want to know now," Sabao begged.

Motatia smiled, "Sabao, all in good timing." She gazed at the two humanoid males showing her evident pride in them.

Radzierians were an advanced civilization of humanoids. They had a complex network of roadways, structures, large cities, and rural developments on the warmer northern hemisphere. The Radzierian humanoids stayed predominantly on the northern side of the planet while the non-humanoid Pulodians inhabited the southern region. Interaction was rare.

"Keyloi, tonight is a good time for you to work on your research assignment. Your father and I have an event at the hospital, and we won't be home until late. Tani Lei will be keeping Contia, so contact her if you need anything. We should be home a few hours after you get here."

"Yes, Tani." His parents frequently had events at the hospital or the school. He always had plenty of things to do himself, and Tani Lei's home was a short distance down the mountain slope from their home. Thankful that Tani Lei was taking care of Contia, Keyloi finally would have some peace from his younger sister for a little while.

***

At a young age, Keyloi learned the basics of medicine from his father. At six years, he could apply healing ointment and bandage small cuts and minor injuries. At eight, he quickly grasped the concept of medicine, and his father stimulated his desire when he took him to his office to observe his medical duties.

"Keyloi, will you bandage the patient's arm while I am administering some medication?" Dad asked his son.

Keyloi felt like a true doctor's assistant as he wrapped a medical bandage around the forearm of one of his patients. He held the bandage with one hand and slowly circled it around the arm. "It's not too tight, is it?" he would ask the 'injured' person. A smile would be on the humanoid's face as they gave the positive answer that he was doing such a great job.

"He will make a fine doctor one day," Dad always complimented.

The regional hospital had many patients from the small surrounding settlements and hamlets. Occasionally, medical physicians from other cities would visit with his father to learn new practices and skills. Keyloi's father held the position of chief medical director for research and development of new techniques. The decades-long influence of the Intergalactic Alliance bolstered his responsibilities and medical practices drastically. He oversaw and taught at two medical universities.

***

The hustaka practice enthused the youths. They planned for their next big event in four days. Sabao practiced on a twisted summersault over Keyloi's head, but his hand slapped his partner's ear. He tried another time, but Keyloi's hand hit Sabao's back. The two thought it would be the best play ever, but they had to perfect it. They were excited about the next practice and pumped up for the tournament.

"Are we going to ever get this?" Keyloi murmured quietly.

"We only have a few days, so we have to keep up the practice," Sabao encouraged.

"Speaking of a few days, I'm about to be eleven. You know what that means," Keyloi bragged.

"Um, you're skipping class?" the best friend knew the answer.

"I'll be older than you," he ribbed.

"Physically by twenty-six days, but mentally, I'm way older than you," came Sabao's response. The two laughed and went to gather their things.

"You remember Mom always lets me spend the night with you so she can get a 'surprise' party ready for me."

"Yea, that's right. Hey, I have the new Mountain Lords game on my Liston Center. We can stay up all night." Discussion and plans started.

***

Keyloi stood at the window of his hillside house that overlooked the city and gazed at the wide ocean that spread for thousands of kilometers. The blue ripples and waves gave an alluring resonance to the atmosphere. Many Busonians were fishers which was a huge industry to the city. He enjoyed watching them as they carried on their business in the water and on shore.

Unlike other planets' green flora from chlorophyll and the cyan shades of Jedira, various hues of red blanketed Radzier. The flora contained anthocyanins which caused the vegetation to have crimson shades.

Fauna abounded with a wide variety of species and subspecies. Mammoth creatures swam in the oceans while others pounded the land. Small mammals scurried around the forest floors, understories, and canopies. Winged creatures gracefully filled the skies.

Keyloi's house overlooked the side of the mountain facing the ocean on the edge of the small metropolis. He gazed at the city of Busonia which was nestled on the lower section of the mountain and oceanfront, or flatland, surrounded by a thick forest of various shades of crimson. The city's hospital snuggled into the middle of the mountainside, almost directly to the west of Keyloi's house. He could see his mother's school just above the flatland below the hospital. He saw Sabao's house directly below his house on the flatland. It was a beautiful city.

He opened the door and stepped out onto his terrace. The air was fresh with few clouds in the sky. The small bay hosted numerous boats of various sizes which dotted the seascape. He loved being on the terrace. It had become his solace when Contia got loud, where he could be alone without distractions.

Keyloi raised his head and noticed the two moons were shining. The largest, Rejaba, hosted the only moon prison for the Intergalactic Alliance, the one all humanoids feared. The smaller satellite, Ceti, meaning Junior, was mainly composed of pure white kaolinite. No larger than three hundred kilometers at the longest point, it shimmered brightly even though the sun shone.

As he leaned on the banister, he felt it quiver. He quickly backed up. *Is it not secured?* He looked at the attachment to the wall. Secure.

Maybe I'm just dizzy from practice. I need to eat something. He realized he hadn't eaten in a while.

He went to the kitchen and took out some bread and scotia spread, grabbed a utensil, and dove into the container.

He felt dizzy once again like the floor moved up.

What is wrong with me?

A large rumble sounded from the open terrace door. He went onto the terrace. Looking toward the hospital, he saw trees, dirt, rocks, and buildings cascading down the mountain. The hospital broke into pieces as it tumbled toward the city below.

Keyloi screamed in terror as he watched the horrific scene. The shaking of his house aggressively increased. The tumbling rocks and sliding trees grew closer to the dwelling. Panic struck the young male as he ran through the house opposite the landslide. He exited the side door as rubble showered his house.

He ran. His heart pounded. His breathing elevated. He

couldn't stop. He ran without looking back. Debris pelted all around him as he used his athletic abilities to run, bounce, jump, dodge, and scurry away from the falling fragments.

After minutes of loud rumbling and non-stop running, piercing pain shot through the back of his head. Lightening bolts rolled in his vision and gave way to gray spots which engulfed his eyesight. He grabbed his head and stumbled. His balance waned as he rolled forward until he felt impact on his body. All went silent.

Section 2

Keyloi blinked open his eyes. He found himself in a small ravine covered with branches and mud. The dust clinging in the air around him caused agonizing pain in his side. He gently touched a painful wet slice on the back of his head. Above that was an extremely sensitive large knot.

He pushed away the debris and struggled to sit up. Pain grabbed his side under his arm and his left temple. He moaned. A self-assessment disclosed no other serious injuries, but the internal pain exploded. Slowly rising to his feet, he kept his eyes closed for a minute to withstand the agony. He wobbled, so he knelt.

As he looked up toward his house, he could see nothing, but land stripped of flora. Some trees still stood around him, but farther on toward where he lived, the land was barren. He slowly got to his feet and tried to walk but stumbled and tripped until he dropped back to his knees. His head pounded, and he felt light-headed. Searching around the ground near him, he found a branch to use as a walking stick. His eyes closed, and he held onto the branch. He needed to breathe, but the clinging dust hampered his progress. He managed to slowly elevate himself until he could stand upright. He made his way through the limb-covered pathway to see if his house still stood. As he eased toward the catastrophe, other views developed.

Upon exiting the partially remaining forest, he realized that he was much lower on the mountain than his house. As he looked for his home, he saw massive devastation in front of him. Nothing stood. No trees, no buildings, no city. Nothing. The closer he moved, the more destruction he saw. He stopped to survey the scene. His mind swirled. He had never seen devastation of that magnitude. He could only stand there and stare. His mind could not grasp the reality of what happened.

The top of the mountain had pushed the whole city down into the ocean clearing everything in its path. All houses and structures from the side of the mountain to the water were gone.

Where is the hospital? Keyloi's heart pounded.

"Mom? Dad?" he let out a helpless yell. He screamed. He cried. The more he viewed the scenery, the worse he felt.

"Tani Lei? Contia?" Tani Lei's house was gone.

Keyloi cried loudly. He called for anyone. No response.

He looked toward the ocean and saw piles of debris on the beaches.

"Sabao?" *No, this can't happen.*

He stood and surveyed the scene for a few seconds longer. Becoming dizzy, he eased himself onto a fallen tree. He stared at the ground. His mind rested.

A mumble sounded. Humanoid. Distant. He faintly heard voices. Something touched his shoulder. He tried to reply but nothing came from his lips. Attempting to look up, his body would not respond.

"Are you okay? Talk to me," came a discernable question.

After a minute, the humanoid lowered him to the ground. His feet were raised. He felt something on his face. Soothing. Keyloi's eyes were open, but he could not focus on any object. A bright light flashed in his eyes.

"He's in shock. We need to get him to triage."

Someone picked him up into their arms and began moving. He felt jostling and movement while being transported.

He wanted to speak but could not. His mind wondered where he was, why he was being moved, who held him, and why he couldn't speak?

His mind grew foggy. He closed his eyes and rested.

***

Keyloi opened his eyes. He could see a ceiling, but not a ceiling. A covering. He was not inside a building. He could hear voices mumbling from two directions. He slowly turned his eyes and moved his head slightly toward one conversation.

"He just moved."

Two people immediately hovered over Keyloi. He looked at both humanoids. He did not recognize them.

"Can you hear me?"

Keyloi just looked at the speaker. He tried to talk, but his words would not come. He blinked.

"If you can hear me, blink two times."

Why was this doctor speaking to me this way? Am I a patient?

"Can you blink two times?" The male looked directly into Keyloi's eyes.

Keyloi gradually blinked twice.

"Yes, he's with us." Surrounding delight lauded.

Why are they talking about me that way?

At that time, a sharp pain blasted through his chest. Keyloi gasped for air. He closed his eyes. He groaned, the first noise his voice made.

"He is still in pain from the broken ribs. Administer a round of dologra."

Minutes after receiving the medicine, Keyloi sighed. He welcomed the quick relief from pain.

"Do you remember what happened?" a kind female voice sounded from his left.

Keyloi moved his eyes toward the questioner. He tried to respond but only garbled noises came out of his mouth.

"Just blink twice for yes and once for no." He felt a hand on his shoulder.

He blinked once. And then again. And then once again. Keyloi did not know how to answer. What was he to remember?

"Very good." The voice quietened as she turned her head. "He answered with three blinks."

"Great. We may assume his cognitive process is still intact."

Keyloi asked what they were talking about. His words were distorted.

The female returned and spoke kindly to him. She told him he was safe and that she would take care of him. When he could speak, she would inform him of current events. She asked a few other questions, but his mind became foggy. His blinks were delayed increasingly, and darkness came over him.

***

He opened his eyes. It was dark. There were two lights in the distance to his left. He stared at the covered ceiling. He moved his head slightly to both sides. He wanted to get up, so he turned to his side. A pain shot through his body. He let out a yell and lay back down.

A female quickly came to his side. She placed her hand on his chest and comforted him.

"You don't need to get up until you completely heal. Can you say anything?"

"Where am I?" Keyloi tried to speak, but his words were slurred.

"I understand it is difficult to speak. We will get you better care as soon as we can. Just rest for now."

Keyloi was confused. He mumbled again. The female

patted his chest.

What is going on? Why can't I speak? What happened? Why won't they tell me anything? This frustrated him. *Why won't they talk to me?*

He lay quietly. Dull pain covered most of his body. His mind ambled from here to there. He tried to think of the past, but everything clouded.

He tried to speak. His words came out garbled. *Why doesn't my mouth work?* He tried repeatedly but nothing understandable surfaced. Finally, he rested.

***

Keyloi opened his eyes. The pain was more than dull but not overwhelming. He heard individuals all around him but at a distance. He called.

"Hello?" It worked. His voice wasn't very loud, but he heard the words.

The comforting female attendant moved closer to him.

"I see you're awake and can speak," came a cheerful voice.

"Where am I?" He mumbled half his words.

"Well, first let's start from right now. How are you feeling?"

"My chest"—Keyloi put his hand over his right side—"and my head hurt."

"That's because you have three broken ribs and a concussion. The doctor has you on pain meds for now, but the

Ossein Cylinder will take care of it as soon as we can transport you to a hospital."

"How did I get hurt?" The words garbled.

"Say that again. Your words are not clear yet," the nurse explained.

Keyloi paused and repeated the words slowly.

"Well, it looks like you were caught in the landslide. You were found on the mountainside at the edge of the forest. You were alone and in shock. What is your name?"

Keyloi pondered her words. *Where was the edge of the forest on the mountainside? What mountainside is she talking about?*

"Um," Keyloi hesitated, "I don't know."

"Do you remember anything about yourself?"

The youth thought but confusion gripped his mind. He repeated, "I don't know."

"Well, listen, we'll take care of you." The kind female comforted him.

Keyloi lay quietly. His mind wondered how he got to the edge of the forest. He did not remember being near a forest. Did the nurse know what she was talking about? He drifted.

***

He could feel himself being moved by bumps and jostles. He heard the loud hum of an engine and felt a lifting sensation as everything moved. He opened his eyes. He could see the sky out the windows of a hilo. He felt the hilo's movement and when it changed directions. He looked around as much as he could, but his eyes seemed heavy, and he quickly wafted into another realm.

***

He heard distant voices. He slowly opened his eyes.

"Hello, young one. How are you feeling?" a young male adult asked.

"Hurting. Where am I?" Keyloi was barely awake and felt light-headed.

"You're in a small hospital unit in Omasciss, and we are going to take care of you for the next few days. I'm Dr. Kelba and this is Nurse Dala. We will be getting you back to health," the doctor said.

Dr. Kelba was a young compassionate male with medium rosy hair and skin. His neatly fashioned hair touched his shoulders. His light green eyes drew Keyloi in as a friend and confidante. He spoke gently to his patient and made him feel comfortable.

An older female with weathered skin and peppered hair, Nurse Dala's touch brought comfort to him.

Keyloi inhaled but pain cut through his chest. "Ahh." He closed his eyes.

"I believe the dologra is about to expire out of your system," the doctor informed him. "And now since you are awake, we can schedule you for the Cylinder to get these injuries repaired."

"Why am I injured?"

"You were injured in the landslide. Do you remember anything that happened?"

Keyloi hesitated. "No."

"Well," the male paused, "I don't think we have discovered who you are. Do you remember your name?"

He looked beyond the doctor and said, "I don't know."

"What about your parents? Do you remember their names?"

Keyloi searched for his thoughts. "No."

"Do you know anything about your life?"

Silence. The doctor and nurse just looked at each other.

Dr. Kelba hesitated, then asked, "Do you remember anything before right now?"

He thought again. "Is something wrong with me?"

The doctor asked, "Do you remember your school?"

"No," Keyloi answered.

"How old are you?" the male asked.

"I'm not sure," He answered after a slight pause.

The doctor looked at Nurse Dala who was beside him, and she shot her eyes at him. Then they returned their attention to their patient. "You don't remember anything at all about yourself?"

"No," he answered.

The doctor paused. He put his hand on Keyloi's forearm and said, "I'll need to do some tests, but I believe you have acute amnesia or memory loss."

Section 3

Keyloi lay quietly. Six days had lapsed since he was hospitalized after the devastating landslide that annihilated the entire city of Busonia. He must have been in Busonia for some reason, but he could not remember. There were only a few dozen survivors. The doctor administered healing with the Ossein Cylinder, and Keyloi felt physically well. Not as well mentally. The hospital provided extensive in-house counseling for the last three days and would provide it if he needed it after being discharged.

He slowly walked to the windows in his hospital room. He peered at the distant mountainside. *Why can't I remember anything? Did I live there? Did I have a mom and dad?* Keyloi was frustrated.

Had he forgotten everything he had ever known? *How can someone lose their memory?* The doctor had explained it to him, but he did not understand.

Dr. Kelba visited often. He handed Keyloi a package of kuper crackers and scotia dip.

"Oh, those are my favorite." Keyloi's eyes widened, and mouth salivated. He had an assemblage of items the doctor brought. He enjoyed the special treatment.

Keyloi met a few other survivors. He didn't recognize any of them. Some had been injured as he had, but others had been out of town and missed the tragedy. All of them lost family members or friends. Everyone remembered the event except Keyloi.

Omasciss, a neighboring city, was about as large as Busonia. Dr. Kelba said that the city hosted the Hemisphere of Hustaka event. Keyloi did not remember what hustaka was, so he wasn't as impressed as the doctor about it. He said the tournament had been cancelled due to the tragedy.

Dr. Kelba administered tests that determined Keyloi had acute amnesia, affecting the memory of his entire previous life. He stated that it wasn't normal, but Keyloi's head injury and concussion damaged his memory center which caused him to forget everything up to that point. He also said it could be temporary or permanent.

"Can't that cylinder fix it?" Keyloi asked.

"Unfortunately, no. The Ossein Cylinder only repairs the physical body. Physically, you are healthy and in very good shape. You must exercise regularly to have your muscle tone. Many children your age do not have a physique like yours," the doctor explained.

"What is my age?"

"I suspect you are around ten or eleven. We won't know until we can find out who you are," he said. "I have some other patients, so do you have any other questions for me before I go?"

"No, I guess not," Keyloi answered.

"Listen, I'll be back soon to check on you. Nurse Dala and the others will take good care of you if you need anything."

"Thank you, Tani," Keyloi responded. He liked the doctor. Keyloi was someone he could trust to take care of him.

After the doctor left, Nurse Dala came to talk with him. "Listen, young one, we cannot keep calling you 'young one.'"

"Why do you call me that?" Keyloi questioned.

She chuckled, "Well, it's because that's what is on your chart. We need to find a temporary name for you, something you would like to be called. Any suggestions?"

Keyloi hadn't thought of a name. He needed one, but what could it be? "No."

"Why don't we come up with a good name for you?" the nurse asked. She said various names, but he wasn't sure which name would be good for him.

After a short time and after comments from other individuals, they arrived at three names that could work: Rala, Forston, and Dorant.

"Why don't you think about those or any others and see if there is one you would like to be called until we discover your real identity?"

Keyloi liked that. He thought of the choices but wasn't sure if they were good names or if he would like any of them. He wanted to get others' opinions first. He asked every individual that came to his room.

Dr. Kelba returned, "How is our young patient?"

"I'm fine. We're trying to think of a name for me. Nurse Dala and the others came up with Rala, Forston, or Dorant. Which do you like best?

"Hm," the doctor pondered. "What about Andaro?"

"Andaro?" Keyloi responded. "Hm. That could work, too."

"I really like Andaro. It matches you."

"Andaro. Andaro. Andaro. I think it sounds good, too," Keyloi said with a smile. "What about a last name?"

"Oh, that will come in time. We'll start calling you Andaro. I love it," he said. "I'll see you later."

"Yes, Tani," Keyloi answered as the doctor disappeared. "Andaro. Yes, that is what I want." He was excited he had a name he could use.

After a little while, Nurse Dala returned. "Thought of anything yet?"

"Yes, Tani. I chose a name," he responded with a glow.

She sat down beside him and asked, "So, what can I call you?"

"Andaro." Keyloi hesitated to make sure she would like the name.

"Andaro? That's a great name. It's perfect for you."

"Dr. Kelba helped me decide," he said.

"You did great. I'm proud of you, Andaro. Someday,

you'll have a last name as well, but that can wait."

Keyloi was happy. A new name all his own. Andaro.

Section 4

Keyloi sat in the back corner of the hospital's dining facility.
That had become his favorite place. Today, he finally had a full
meal. Other humanoids sat at surrounding tables.

He had been informed that he would be moved to a
temporary family until suitable assistance could be rendered for
him. Concerned about his future, he wondered if he would ever
make friends. Just then, the conversation between two males
behind his bench grabbed his attention. They were speaking
quietly of the tragedy.

"The Busonian death toll stands at forty-three thousand,
six hundred. That does not consider the number of medical
personnel and staff who were at the hospital for the annual event,
nor just individual visitors to the city. There could have easily
been fifty thousand killed. It was the worst disaster the planet has
ever had. I believe only a few dozen citizens survived."

"Such a tragic loss to our medical world. The Alliance
invested so much in the facility, and the loss of Dr. Kontes was
such a disaster. One of the greatest medical minds of our time."

Sadness touched Keyloi's heart that a famous doctor had

been killed.

"Have you talked to every survivor? We need to have that information," the doctor questioned the younger male.

"Yes, all but two children. One is an infant, so there's little chance there. The other is a young boy. It's hard to get information on minors. He may know something."

Keyloi held his breath.

"What? Where is he?" The younger of the two spoke in a lower voice.

"He may be at this facility or another hospital. He may have already been placed in temporary care. It's difficult to say," the young male explained.

I will check the schedule here. I may find his location if he was here and has been placed in the community," the doctor replied.

Keyloi's heartbeat and breathing increased. He heard quiet, unrecognizable mumbles from the adults. He turned away and slumped down deeper in his chair. *Why are they looking for me? What do I know? Were my family criminals?*

Then the two males got up and exited the room without seeing Keyloi.

He watched them leave, slowly got up, and walked toward the exit, leaving his dishes and utensils on the table. He peered around both corners into the hallway but did not see the two males. He quickly walked toward his room to hide. As he neared the corner, he heard the two in the adjoining hallway.

"Is he at this hospital, and this his room?"

"Yes, but there's no one here."

"You wait for him. I'll go check his chart for any therapy schedule or placement assignment." The adult wearing a doctor's jacket walked away. He exited down the hallway away from Keyloi. Keyloi's mind searched what he needed to do. He turned and ran to his counselor's office. She was with another patient.

Nurse Dala? Dr. Kelba?

As he left the office, the adult entered. Keyloi slipped around him and slowly walked down the hallway. He heard the door close, looked behind him, and saw no one there. He ran. He found the staircase and quickly ran up to find Dr. Kelba. He found the doctor's office and opened the door. The doctor and nurse were both seated inside the office having a discussion.

"I need help," Keyloi gasped for air.

The two quickly looked up. Dr. Kelba asked, "What's the problem?"

"What do I do if someone is hunting for me?"

The doctor motioned for him to close the door and come closer. "What are you talking about?"

"Someone is looking for me. I don't know them."

"How do you know this?" the doctor asked.

"I overheard them talking in the cafeteria about the tragedy and were wondering if they had talked to all the survivors. They needed information. They looked serious."

"About what?"

"I don't know. One said he had talked to everyone but a baby and a boy. They left to find me. I went to my room, but they were outside the door. I ran to my counselor's office, but they were there, too."

"Hmm," Dr. Kelba looked around. "Why don't you stay in here? I'll make sure no one knows you're here." He locked the door and showed Keyloi a chair.

Keyloi calmed. He settled in the chair and searched the adults' faces for help.

"Nurse Dala, will you check the hallway and make sure nothing is out of the ordinary?" He turned to Keyloi. "What did these two look like?"

Keyloi described the two individuals as well as he could to the doctor.

"So, it sounds like from what they were wearing that at least one of them is a doctor? Hmm, I don't recognize them by the description. I wish I had more information. I'll ask around. But until then, you stay right here."

Keyloi felt comfortable staying there.

The nurse returned but found nothing. The doctor asked if she recognized anyone from Keyloi's description. He asked the lad to give her details. She did not have an answer.

The doctor took out his databoard and input some data. "I'm contacting Child Protection for help." After a moment, Dr. Kelba stated that they instructed him to take Keyloi to a secure location for temporary protection.

"Andaro, they will take care of you. If you have any problems, you make sure one of us know," Nurse Dala spoke, her tone serious. "We want you protected."

"Thank you, Tani." He could feel the warmth of both adults.

"Now, we just need to get you out of the hospital and into my vehicle without anyone seeing you," Dr. Kelba stated.

"Let me see what I can do to find some street clothing," Nurse Dala said as she left the room.

The doctor patted Keyloi on the shoulder and said, "You're safe with us."

Nurse Dala soon returned with a bag.

Dr. Kelba asked the nurse, "Will you check the hallway toward the west staircase? I'm parked just outside that door. We'll get everything ready to leave."

"Where are you taking him," she asked.

"The agency gave me a location. I'll get with them for further guidance."

She left the room with Keyloi and the doctor in his office.

The doctor pulled some clothing out of the bag. "Change into these." He gave Keyloi the clothing. Keyloi hesitated, looked around the room, and then changed into his escape clothing. He felt awkward with the doctor in the room watching him.

"Hey, and I have something else for you," the doctor went to his desk and pulled out a Hemisphere of Hustaka knit hat.

"That's nice. Thank you, Tani," he responded.

"I got it for the event, but then they canceled. I'm glad to give it to you," he said. As Keyloi was snapping his shirt, the doctor pulled it over his head tucking Keyloi's hair behind his ears.

The doctor looked him over and said, "You look great. Now, let's get out of here."

They went to the door, and the doctor looked both ways in the hallway. He saw Nurse Dala waving near the staircase. He motioned to Keyloi, and they entered the hall toward their destination.

"Just stay with me, and do not act afraid. No matter who or what you see," he whispered with a serious expression. "Act like you belong with me."

"Yes, Tani," Keyloi said with hesitation.

They passed a few individuals without incident as they neared the end of the hallway. In the staircase, they descended to the lower levels and to the exit. The doctor blocked him from the door as he opened and investigated. Soon, they were in the vehicle and driving away.

Section 5

After a little drive away from town, they turned off the main road onto a private road. Crimson trees enveloped the road with multi-colored flowers lining the very long driveway. They entered the courtyard, and the doctor drove into a garage. Exiting the vehicle, they entered the structure through a side door.

The doctor's home astonished Keyloi. Plenty of windows allowed beautiful rays, providing natural lighting. Nice decor and design in every room. Multileveled platforms held various pieces of furniture. One of those levels hosted a Liston Center with a large screen display on the right of the room.

"Do you remember a Liston Center?" the doctor inquired.

"Um, no." Keyloi was puzzled.

"Amnesia is a crazy thing. You may remember some things but may not remember anything. Every case is different." The doctor patted him on his back. "You can use it any time. Just make yourself at home here."

Keyloi looked up and answered, "Yes, Tani." He didn't know how to fully express his gratitude to the doctor for keeping him safe. "Thank you."

"Oh, of course. Over here will be your room." He opened the bedroom door.

Keyloi walked inside, and the elegant furnishings impressed him. He looked at himself in the mirror, explored the closets, and found an adjoining room. His own private relieving room.

"Will this be good for you?"

"Yes, this is nice, Tani."

"Good. I'll bring you some more clothing tomorrow."

"Thank you, Tani." Keyloi was dazed by the provisions. The peaceful home provided whatever he needed, from protection to entertainment.

Dr. Kelba guided him to a room at the back of the house filled with exercise equipment of all kinds, a small exercise pad, a wall-mounted screen for entertainment, and two other pieces of furniture that needed to be explored.

"Max!" Keyloi said in a quiet voice.

"Come on in here, and I'll show you the kitchen," Dr. Kelba said as he started in that direction. Keyloi followed toward a concave section on the other side of the central room. There were a few cabinets, a water dispenser, and a food replicator.

"Are you hungry?"

"Yes, Tani." He had not eaten since at cafeteria, so he looked to see what might be available. The doctor ordered him a small meal, and within a minute a pleasant tune sounded, indicating the food was prepared. He opened the small door and removed a steamy bowl. Keyloi wasn't sure what it had generated, but the smell of the warm rising vapors made his mouth salivate. The doctor ordered his meal, and they sat at a comfortable table dining and made small talk.

"Andaro, I am so sorry about what you have had to go through in the past few months. It's unfair that someone your age should have to deal with all this. I will see what I can do to make things go well for you and to find out who you are.

"Thank you, Tani."

"How has counseling been for you?"

Keyloi felt genuine concern pouring from the doctor. He longed to keep that feeling forever. He admired him and was glad they found each other. He caught himself staring at the adult. "Um, it's going well, Tani," Keyloi responded.

"I'll need to work something out to continue your sessions without you going back to the hospital. I want to keep you away from those who want to harm you."

"Thank you, Tani."

After their meal, Keyloi asked about the Liston Center.

"Andaro, consider this your home, and you can use the Center any time you wish."

"Will you show me how?"

"Of course." Dr. Kelba rose to visit the Center.

After a few instructions, the youth explored, but as he searched, he thought of how wonderful the doctor had been to him. He was happy.

Before the doctor retired for the night, he told Keyloi to enjoy himself and that he wouldn't wake him in the morning when he left for the hospital.

"Thank you, Tani." Keyloi envisioned what he could do around the house.

"When I'm gone to work, you will be safe inside, so do not exit or open the doors for anyone. That's kind of important. The alarm system will alert law enforcement and me and everyone will be here. We don't want that to happen."

"No, Tani. Thank you," Keyloi glanced around the room. After the doctor went to his room, Keyloi looked around the Center and found a few areas he would like to view but thought he would wait until tomorrow.

***

Keyloi opened his eyes. He rested well in a comfortable bed. He smelled whisps in the air that had an alluring scent. He sat up and looked around the room. He went to the relieving room and cleaned up. Afterward, he returned to the bedroom and stretched his legs and arms. He stood and went to the mirror to examine his appearance. Sitting on the dresser below the mirror were some folded clothes that had not been there when he went to sleep. He picked them up to find a hustaka-themed outfit. Surprised, he put on the shorts and shirt. They fit well and looked nice on him. "Max," he whispered.

He stopped. Hustaka pricked his memory. *Do I have memories of hustaka?* He tried to focus on a sport he knew nothing about. Nothing surfaced.

Keyloi exited the bedroom and looked around the central room. The scent flurried his nostrils stronger than ever. A memory flashed from this aroma. In a kitchen, he worked with an adult woman. She handed him some toast and said, "Here, Keyloi." Spread covered the bread. The memory vanished. *Who was she?*

He pondered the vague memories for a moment then went to the kitchen and found Dr. Kelba. The aroma: warm scotia and toasted bread.

"That smells good," Keyloi savored the fragrance. "Good morning, Tani. I keep getting little bits of memories that I don't remember. Do you think it is of my past?"

"Good morning, Andaro. Just keep trying to remember. Maybe it will all come back some day," Dr. Kelba greeted with a big smile.

"I heard the name Keyloi. Does that mean anything?"

"Keyloi? No, I don't know anyone by that name. I can search it and see," Dr Kelba suggested.

"Thank you, and thank you for the clothes," Keyloi said politely.

"Of course. They look good on you. I heard you when you awoke and prepared what Nurse Dala said was your favorite." The doctor gestured to the breakfast.

"Thank you, Tani. I thought you were going to be at the hospital today," Keyloi replied looking at the meal with a gleam in his eye. He sat down and tantalized his tastebuds.

"I thought I'd stay here with you this morning. Do you battle with the Lavaheads?" he gave a big smile.

Keyloi was confused about the term. "What's a Lavahead?"

"Oh, yeah," he hesitated. "They are creatures in the game of Mountain Lords. It's not difficult. You finish your breakfast, I'll show you how to play." The doctor went to the Liston Center to get the game started.

Keyloi's curiosity soared about the game. Dr. Kelba explained everything. He thought the doctor was the greatest.

***

Loads of cheers erupted. "Did you let me win?" Keyloi asked his competitor.

A faux shocked look came across the doctor's face as he placed his hand on his chest. "I would never!"

They both laughed and enjoyed their time together as much as they played the game.

"Oh, no. I forgot what time it was. I must get to the hospital." He jumped up to go to his room to ready himself.

Keyloi watched the doctor leave. He really liked him. He was glad he met him and allowed him to stay at with him at his home. A sense of peace covered him like he had not experienced. He was happy.

After a few minutes, Dr. Kelba came out of his room. "Enjoy your day, and I'll see you in a few hours. Remember, stay inside."

"Okay, I will, Tani," Keyloi responded.

The doctor departed and locked the door.

Keyloi sat back on the sofa. He inhaled deeply and slowly released the air. He took some time to reflect on his past. He could remember being in pain at the hospital, but now he enjoyed a beautiful home with a wonderful provider.

That evening, Dr. Kelba brought two new outfits for Keyloi. The youth changed into each set and fashioned them for the doctor who praised each one.

"You model clothes well. It's all those muscles you have," Dr. Kelba commented.

Keyloi examined the clothing he adorned. They were extremely comfortable and looked good on him. "Thank you, Tani."

Days passed. When the doctor returned home, he always brought something Keyloi enjoyed. Sometimes a small gadget, sometimes a piece of clothing. Each item seemed to be just what Keyloi enjoyed. He wondered why the doctor always brought gifts to him. He appreciated them, and they helped occupy his time in the doctor's absence.

One day he asked, "Why do you bring me something every day?"

"Do you not like what I bring you?"

"Oh, no, I love them and thank you for everything. You do so much for me."

"Listen, Andaro"—the doctor put his hand on Keyloi's upper arm—"you've been through so much loss recently I want to help you settle in well. And besides, I can spend my famols any way I want." He grinned and raised an eyebrow.

Keyloi chuckled. "Thank you, Tani. Just staying in your home is nice," Keyloi gestured around the room as he spoke.

"I'm glad you're happy staying here." He released his arm and patted the lad's shoulder. "Now, when are we ever going to get rid of those Lavaheads?"

Keyloi smiled. He loved playing the game, and Dr. Kelba was such a fun partner.

Section 6

After a hearty game of Mountain Lords and calming down from the excitement, the doctor said, "Andaro, I want to discuss something with you. You've been living here with me for the last two weeks or so. Have you ever considered living with me permanently and allowing me to adopt you as my son?"

Keyloi was speechless. Adopted? That sounded serious. But with no family, he would need to be adopted. He had never thought of being adopted, much less by whom. He liked the doctor and loved staying in his home.

"You don't have to answer that question now. Why don't you think about it, and we can discuss it later. Until then, you are welcome to stay here. The house will keep you safe as long as you don't open the door."

Keyloi realized he didn't answer. "Does anyone know where I am?" Keyloi questioned.

Dr. Kelba thought for a minute. "I spoke with Child Protection about you staying here, and they agreed to officially place you here. I did mention adoption to them, and they thought that my adopting you would be the best thing for you. So, only those in their agency who need to know have been told. Nurse Dala just knows that I took you somewhere to be safe."

"When can I go outside the house?"

"Well, I have a Tymina House. That means that the house was built around a security system. Any intrusion would set off the alarm and everything would immediately secure itself. That's why I keep asking you to stay inside and not open any doors," the doctor explained.

"Did you ever find out who was looking for me?"

"That, I did not. There are hundreds of medical personnel at the hospital, so I needed a better description."

"Sorry, that's all I could remember," Keyloi apologized.

"But I did find out that a group is searching for you. I don't know how many humanoids are involved, but they are actively asking questions around the hospital. I have avoided answering their questions, but they are getting aggressive in their search.

"So, if you adopted me, would I still be safe?"

"I think I can protect you from them. That's why I asked if you would agree for me to adopt you," the doctor explained. "If you are not safe around here, we will move to another location. I'll do anything to keep you safe."

"Thank you, Tani."

Keyloi stared at the doctor. He liked him, enjoyed living in his home, and always felt safe and happy there. He finally answered, "Yes, Tani, will you adopt me?"

A big smile came upon Dr. Kelba's face. "Absolutely, I will. That makes me so happy, Andaro. I'll start on the paperwork tomorrow."

Keyloi was excited. He would have a place he could call home with a father he already loved.

Section 7

Keyloi opened his eyes. He rested well. His thoughts returned to the previous evening's discussion about adoption. He loved the thought of joining Dr. Kelba as a family.

He rose and completed his routine preparation for the day. He went to the kitchen to find something to generate. There were so many items on the menu, and he wanted to try them. He had started at the top, and the menu for that day was number twenty. Today, the warm breakfast did not taste as good as other items he had gotten. *I won't be getting this one again.*

He walked into the central room and looked around. He went to the back exercise room and played around on the hustaka loops. He performed certain maneuvers so easily it surprised him. He really liked doing hustaka and planned on asking Dr. Kelba about joining a team someday. He went to the other machines and tried to discover how they worked. After a few hours of inspecting all the equipment, he returned to the central room. He looked at the Liston Center but wanted to do something different. His eyes fell on Dr. Kelba's bedroom door.

I wonder what his bedroom is like. He walked to the door

he had never entered. He slowly opened the door to reveal a very spacious and beautifully designed room. The bed sat on a raised platform with steps to the landing. There were floor-to-ceiling windows surrounding the room as the outside wall. A concave of mirrors surrounded a dressing cabinet. Two doors revealed a relieving room and closet.

He walked around to look at the surroundings. He saw a small sitting area with covers draped over the backs of the two chairs. Behind the chairs, a door led to the outside. He went to the windows and peered out toward the back landscape. The wooded scenery welcomed peace. He remembered being surrounded by trees as he walked down a pathway with someone. Another boy. The memory stopped.

He pondered the flashback. *Who was this boy?* He continued searching the woods to try to resurface the memory, but he had no success.

A small four-legged creature came from behind one of the large trees. Covered in dark crimson fur, its short neck and legs made the fauna entertaining to watch. It sniffed around, looked up to the left of the house, and returned to investigate the ground. Keyloi watched it roam around the edge of the woods and then scurry back into the forest. He was impressed to see nature in the wild.

Closer to the house, the grounds were well manicured. On his right side against the house sat a child's playset. *What is that?* He pressed his face against the window but could only see a small section of it. *Why would there be a child's toy here? I didn't know Dr. Kelba had children. He has never said anything about them.*

He continued looking around but tried not to pry into his closet or cabinets. He just wanted to explore every room of the house.

He exited the bedroom into the exercise room. He went again to the mats and began some hustaka moves. He powered on the screen and found a hustaka tournament. He watched with intensity as they performed their moves. *I can do that.* He would pause the performance to do the move then resume the competition.

He hadn't realized how long he had been practicing until he heard the door open in the central room. He went to look, and Dr. Kelba had just arrived.

"Hey, Andaro, how was your day?" came the cheerful greeting.

"Great. I did some hustaka moves just like the ones on the screen," he answered excitedly.

"I bet you can perform as well as they do," the doctor replied.

Keyloi chuckled. "Can I join a team?"

"You would be great on one, but let's make sure you are safe first."

"Oh, yeah," he remembered. "Did you check into the adoption?"

"I did start the adoption paperwork. They said it will take a month or two to get things settled, and then you will be Andaro Kelba." The doctor glowed with pride.

"Andaro Kelba. I like that name." Keyloi smiled at how it sounded.

"I'll look into local hustaka teams, and you'll have to show me your moves."

"Max!" Keyloi replied. "You want to see right now?"

"Let me clean up from work and let's have dinner first, and then give me the show," Dr. Kelba said with a big smile.

***

Keyloi didn't realize how hungry the exercise made him. He asked for seconds.

"Help yourself. You're good at working the replicator, and there's no reason to be hungry."

Dinner was nice. They cleaned their tableware, and Dr. Kelba said, "Now, show me what you know about hustaka."

Keyloi smiled. They moved to the gym, and he jumped to grab the handles. He started twists, turns, flips, and rolls. The maneuvers were simple to him.

"You really are a natural," the doctor commented. Keyloi smiled. He continued with a few more moves.

"You are really fit and muscular for your age. You look good."

Keyloi did a final flip and landed on his feet. He glowed with pride.

"Wow, great performance." Dr. Kelba patted his shoulder. "And look at those muscles. You have a good physique."

"That was fun." Keyloi glowed.

"Maybe we can find a team some day when you're safe." The doctor put his arm around Keyloi's shoulders.

"I would like that. Thank you, Tani."

They returned to the central room when Keyloi saw the doctor's bedroom door. "Oh, today I saw a little fauna walk out of the forest. It was cute and furry.

"Oh, that sounds like a limya, the doctor replied. "There are a few in the forest that come around at times. Many families have them as small pets or comfort animals."

He then remembered the playset. "Oh, I have a question."

"Ask away," Dr. Kelba replied.

"Have you ever had children?"

The doctor was visibly stumped. The smile dropped from his face. He removed his arm from Keyloi's shoulders, lowered his head, and became quiet.

"I'm sorry if I offended you." Keyloi felt like he shouldn't have asked the question. "I saw a playset in the back yard and was wondering because I hadn't seen any children around, and you hadn't mentioned it."

"It's okay, Andaro. How did you see the playset?"

Keyloi felt cornered. He had to admit he entered the adult's room. "I'm sorry, Tani, but I went into your bedroom. I wanted to see all around the house, and I had never seen your room. I looked out the window and saw it in the backyard. I'm sorry I went into your room."

"Andaro, it's okay to go into my bedroom. I don't hide anything in there." He paused for a moment. "Yes, I have … had a daughter. She and her mother were in Busonia during the landslide."

Keyloi was devastated. "I'm so sorry, Tani," Keyloi heart dropped. He decided he would not ask any more questions about his family.

"It's okay, Andaro, I miss them dearly." The doctor recovered. "But I have to move on as you are doing."

Keyloi was quiet. He had not heard the doctor speak of his family before now. *He recovered well and quickly from the disaster. By being his son, I can help him.* Keyloi comforted himself by that thought.

Section 8

A week later, Dr. Kelba returned home early. "Andaro! Where are you?"

Keyloi came from the exercise room and greeted him.

"Listen, the ones who were searching for you, know you are with me, and they are on their way here. We must leave now." The doctor breathed heavily.

A tinge of fear hit Keyloi. "Where are we going?"

"Gather your things and let's go," Dr. Kelba said as he went toward his bedroom.

Keyloi ran into his room and grabbed his clothing and hygiene items. He stuffed them into a garment bag and returned to the central room. He heard the doctor mumbling to himself while making noises in his bedroom.

"Can I help?" Keyloi called out from the open door.

"Keep watch out the windows to see if anyone comes close to the house. I'll be there in a minute."

Keyloi went to the front windows and kept a steady watch for anything that moved. *Won't we be safe in the house? If no one can get in, why are we leaving?*

Soon, Dr. Kelba returned and asked if he saw anything. "No, Tani."

"Let's get moving," the doctor said as he surveyed the outside scene. He unlocked the front door, and they entered the garage for the vehicle. They quickly secured themselves inside the vehicle. The doctor opened the garage door and drove out. He used his databoard to initiate safety procedures at the house. Keyloi saw shutters sliding down over the windows and doors. The vehicle quickly drove away.

"That will keep anyone away from the house until we can return," Dr. Kelba stated.

There was no conversation as the adult drove through the countryside for many kilometers away from the city. The picturesque landscape was beautiful with its scenic mountains and valleys. The road wound through umbrellas of crimson trees. Fauna mingled around some of the tree trunks near a pasture.

Finally, Keyloi broke the silence and asked, "Why did we leave the house if no one can get in?"

The doctor paused. "Well … uh … we couldn't stay inside forever without getting out at least for supplies. They would have watched the house day and night until we left." He looked at Keyloi and put his hand on the boy's knee. "Andaro, I want to keep you safe."

Keyloi glanced at the doctor's hand. "Thank you, Tani."

After a few more kilometers, Keyloi broke the silence when he asked, "Where are we going?"

"Oh, I'm sorry, Andaro. I was deep in thought. We're going to a colleague's home in Baxing Hills."

Keyloi had never heard of that place, so he returned his gaze out the windows. After a few minutes, he asked, "Will I be safe there?"

The doctor glanced over at him. He patted Keyloi's knee and said, "I'll keep you safe, Son?" He turned back to the roadway.

Keyloi continued staring at him. *Son?* That was so foreign to him. He wanted to be part of a family, and he really liked Dr. Kelba and wanted to be his son. On the other hand, hearing himself being called 'son' seemed to distance himself from whatever past he may have. *I can get used to it,* he assured himself.

He realized he was still staring, and he quickly replied, "Thank you, Tani." He looked back outside the window.

After thirty minutes, Dr. Kelba pulled off the road onto a pathway through the grasses. He drove for a few hundred meters until they came to a covering of trees.

"We can get out here. It's just down the way." The doctor opened the door. Keyloi followed. The vehicle parked under a canopy of trees within an arching cover of camouflage mesh that closed behind the vehicle. He had never seen such a disguise.

"It's just a short walk there."

Keyloi was intrigued by the stealth.

They followed a walkway that domed in shades of red.

The beautiful footpath was mostly level and covered in a canopy of crimson. The route twisted and turned then straightened again. Keyloi kept up a steady pace.

"Tani? Where are we going?"

After slight hesitation, Dr. Kelba responded. "We're heading to a safe place." The doctor never missed a step as he spoke. His eyes continually scanned the area as he trod.

"How much farther?"

"Not much."

The two continued down the path, through the forest, over a fallen log, and onto another pathway. Finally, they ended up in a dell with a group of rocks. It appeared large rocks had fallen from the sheer cliff just behind them. Dr. Kelba sat to rest. Keyloi sat beside him. Trees covered the surroundings to block out the blue-painted sky. It was peaceful. Keyloi could hear the forest fauna sounding their calls and songs. The quiet sound of running water to their left. Various delicate aromas wafted into his nostrils.

"Wait." Keyloi looked around and gasped.

Dr. Kelba stopped and turned to see what had happened.

"I've been here. Or maybe a place like this." He continued looking at the cerise covering. "I was with someone. Another boy."

"Uh, we need to hurry," the doctor looked concerned and took his arm. "I'm sure it's just a pseudo-memory. Those can happen with amnesia patients. I wouldn't dwell too much on it."

Keyloi could not help but dwell on it. It felt like a memory from his old life.

Dr. Kelba surveyed the area and took out his databoard. He punched a few buttons and waited. He stood and told Keyloi to stand. He then faced the cliff and placed both palms down on the top of the rock for a few seconds where they had rested. He then grabbed the front side of the rock at his knees and lifted. The rocks easily folded back into the cliff wall to reveal a staircase underneath the cliff.

"Max!" Wide-eyed, Keyloi saw the operation develop. "Are you part of the R.I.D. or something like that?"

Dr. Kelba chuckled. "Yes, something like that. You probably mean the R.I.E., the Regional Intelligence Enforcement. We protect humanoids from being victims."

That information made Keyloi feel safe.

"Follow me." Dr. Kelba took off down the stairs. Keyloi stayed on his heels.

As they passed the entrance going down the stairs, the doorway quietly closed, and the staircase lit up as they progressed. He stepped downward for another seven meters then leveled into a small room that was illuminated by indirect lighting. The walls were painted with soft colors that made the atmosphere welcoming. Decorations enhanced the overall appearance. An exit glowed on the opposite side of the room. Dr. Kelba opened the door and led Keyloi inside.

The doctor gave a grand tour of the facility. The central

room was a good size but not too large, nicely decorated, furnished with a couch, two comfortable-looking chairs, a Liston Center with a large, mounted monitor, and cabinets in the corner. In the far end of the room, a food preparation area hosted a food replicator and counter with two chairs. There were three doors along the walls which led to two other rooms, each with a bed, table, wall lamp, and shelf. The third opened into a relieving room. The residence was small but comfortable.

The doctor finally spoke. "This will be our home for a little while until I can work out other arrangements. It's too dangerous for you, and me now, to be in public."

"I'm sorry for getting you in trouble." Keyloi thought for a moment. "Can't you just go to the authorities? Wouldn't they help?"

"Andaro, you don't worry about me. And the authorities are in on this," came a serious response.

Fear covered the youth. "If the authorities are searching for us, what are we going to do?"

The doctor gestured for them to have a seat. "I've been thinking about that. We need to leave from around here. We can move somewhere far away and never be bothered with those humanoids again." He looked at his databoard then put it down. "So where would you like to live if you could live anywhere on Radzier or in the multiverse?"

Keyloi stared at his new father. He had never thought of living anywhere in particular.

The doctor saw the youth's hesitation. "Why don't we discuss this?"

The youth just stared at him.

"Have you ever thought of traveling to another planet?"

"No."

"What about going into outer space? Don't you think it would be great to live in a world you've never been to before? We wouldn't have to worry about anyone looking for us."

Keyloi thought for a moment. "I don't know. Where?"

"Well"—the doctor looked back at his databoard—"there's Earth, but it is very crowded. Eden is a beautiful planet where the Intergalactic Alliance headquarters is located, but it also is getting heavily populated. Then there is Bliteque, but we would need to wear translators to understand the inhabitants. Proxima b could be an option. Jedira has a few new colonies with lots to explore. I hear they are growing and will probably have a hustaka team by now."

"Do you think so?" Keyloi perked up.

"I'm sure they do. Hustaka is a growing activity. If they don't have anything like it, I'll help you get a group started." His large smile tantalized the youth.

"That would be great." Keyloi's emotions jumped. He was excited to learn more about the sport and being on a team.

"Maybe you could become one of the hustaka instructors," the doctor encouraged.

Keyloi's mind exploded with ideas. *It does come easy for*

me. He said I was a natural, and I might learn enough to be an instructor. I know all the routines and could learn more.

"Yes, let's go to Jedira," Keyloi erupted with anticipation.

"I think that would be the best place. Let me check into some things, and I'll start getting ready for it. I'm excited for you."

"I am, too. I'll keep practicing the moves and try to learn more." The thought of the sport and opportunity to travel to another planet excited him. He knew life was going to change, and he looked forward to it.

Section 9

The trip to Jedira continued long and uneventful. Keyloi talked with his adoptive father about their future at Jedira. He spent most of his time in the Green or Red Rooms. The Green Room contained the activity room with games and challenges for individuals and teams while the Red Room had a theater and various Liston Centers. Their designs entertained young travelers on long space travel between inhabited planets.

"Andaro?" Keyloi felt a hand on his shoulder. "Why haven't you responded when I called?"

The youth had temporarily forgotten the pseudonym. "Uh, I am sorry, Tani. I was watching this match. They are good." He had been watching a recent Hustaka match from the Radzierian games.

"First, why don't you call me Dad? I am your adopted father," the doctor asked curiously. Dr. Kelba announced the adoption just before they left Radzier.

Keyloi thought for a moment. He could do that. "I'm sorry, T ... Dad." He smiled.

Dr. Kelba put his arm around his shoulders and said, "It's

okay. In time you will get used to it." He gave his adopted son a big smile. "Have you forgotten to eat again?"

Keyloi thought and smiled. "I guess I have."

"Finish up here, and let's go get something. You need to stay strong and healthy for your practices when we get to our new home."

"Okay. Let me reset this." Keyloi closed out the video on the Liston Center and followed his father to the cafeteria.

They enjoyed a meal and their time together. They discussed all they could do and learn at their new home and the new sights and humanoids they will meet.

"Since we have always been on Radzier, you will see many humanoid species with other skin, hair, and eye colors and some that don't look like us. In a colony, there will be humanoids from various planets, races, and species like you see on this ship," Dr. Kelba stated. "I have searched information on various humanoid species and found a wide variety. There are those with very light skin and others who are very dark. Those from Bliteque have purple skin and wear translators to communicate."

"Wow, that's different." Keyloi thought of what that would look like.

"Yeah, here are some photos." The doctor showed him a few images of inhabitants from the four other planets. "The multiverse is so different from Radzier. We need to learn about others before we encounter them. No matter what a person looks like or where they are from, remember that they are an individual with feelings, desires, and needs. We must always respect them as equal individuals and not inferior to us."

"Yes, Tani," the lad responded as he reviewed the photos. "When can I get my own databoard? I want to research, too."

"Well," the doctor started, "multiversal law is fourteen. You still have a couple more years. We established you as twelve years."

"Why can't we establish me as fourteen?"

"Andaro?" The doctor tilted his head and smiled.

"That's not fair. Who makes those laws?"

Dr. Kelba laughed aloud. "That's a Radzierian law as well. I don't really know who creates them. Probably representatives from all planets get together. Who knows?"

Keyloi accepted his answer. The two continued reviewing photos and descriptions of the various cultures and customs from other planets.

During their scheduled sleep, Keyloi dug around in his bag and came across his identification documents. He smiled. He opened his passport to see his photo and the name Andaro Gravton. He remembered the doctor explaining that they needed to change their last name so no one could find them. He liked Kelba better, but Gravton would do. His adopted father had joined the Alliance as a doctor which sped up the process of their departure to Jedira. He was excited about their new journey.

Section 10

The captain announced that they were approaching the Jediran space portal and everyone could view the planet out the port side. "Jedira is the newest of the six known habitable planets in the multiverse, and the first to be inhabited completely from other planets. This solar system is in the Capria-Bateli Quadrant, and Jedira is the second planet from the sun, Capria. If you notice a cyan hue to the planet, well, this is because the plant-life on Jedira is cyan or has a bluish tint."

Keyloi jumped up to look. He moved to the left portholes and observed a bluish covered sphere.

"If you notice the two satellites orbiting Jedira, these are the planet's two moons. The largest is Wilstor and the smallest is Kadyen. One interesting note is that these two bodies circle the planet in opposite directions. No need to worry. Their orbit is far enough apart to not cross each other's path, so there is no concern about colliding moons while you are here." The captain's voice was professional and comfortable, explaining details with humor. "We will be docking at the space portal within the hour, and you should be able to debark soon thereafter.

Thank you for taking this voyage with us, and we hope your time on Jedira is delightful."

Excitement saturated the air as the visitors anticipated their departure. Discussions and movements increased as the passengers gathered their belongings. The spacecraft slowly maneuvered to the entry point of the space portal. Keyloi felt small bumps, but no other notable adjustments could be detected.

The two made their way off the vessel and to the space portal floor. Within the next hour, passengers had completely departed and had moved toward their final destinations. Humanoids were bustling everywhere as if they knew their terminus. Most travelers were bound for the planet while a few were moving on to other spacecrafts toward more distant planets and locations.

The two looked around to see where they should go. Dr. Kelba pointed to the left and said, "Let's go that way."

Keyloi grabbed his luggage handle and pulled it behind him as he followed his adoptive father. Soon, they arrived at the counter for their final journey to the planet. The attendant asked many questions as the doctor answered kindly. Keyloi took in the scenes and tried not to stare at the various shades of skin. He was intrigued at the world he had entered.

"Andaro," the doctor said, "she needs to see your identification. Do you have it with you?"

Keyloi displayed his passport. After showing their identifications, they headed to an air shuttle about to depart to the planet.

Looking outside the shuttle's porthole, Keyloi watched everything. He saw individuals as they hurried around the dock looking for where they needed to be. The portal doors were about to open for departure, so the flight deck was evacuated. An alarm sounded, and within two minutes, the massive doors slowly opened to reveal a void of blackness. Slowly, the air shuttle made its way outside the doors and drifted for a few moments. Soon, speed garnered, and the shuttle blasted off toward its spherical destination.

Along the way, the shuttle captain began, "Welcome to Jedira. We will be landing at the Jediran air portal in approximately two hours. The portal is located outside Alpha Colony which is the headquarters for the four satellite colonies on the planet. After Jedira's climatization, Alpha Colony was founded a few decades ago for habitation as an outpost and for colonization. As far as it is known, there are currently no fauna on the planet. Soil makeup causes the flora to have a cyan hue, similar to the greens and reds on other planets. The air is breathable for all humanoids. Temperatures fluctuate little daily and throughout the year. Another interesting fact is that it does not rain on Jedira. Nightly mists rise from the ground and give the vegetation its needed nourishment. We will be landing shortly, so please return to your seats. We trust you have enjoyed your short flight with us this afternoon."

The air shuttle trip arrived without incident. Through the

porthole, Keyloi saw the approaching city where they would land. A large building rested outside the colony near a landing pad.

"Now, remember"—Dr. Kelba turned to Keyloi and whispered—"you are Andaro Gravton. I am Trodner Gravton. Don't forget. There are humanoids assigned all over the multiverse who could be looking for you, so help me keep you safe."

"Yes, Tani"—Keyloi answered—"I mean Dad." He shrugged. Dr. Kelba chuckled.

After a smooth landing, the shuttle unloaded in front of the administration building. All passengers took their luggage and walked into the edifice.

"We are assigned to Alpha Colony, so we need to find out where we will live and where my work and your school are located."

Internally, Keyloi struggled but prepared himself for the new venture. This new experience for him kept his structured mind alert.

The two caught a ground shuttle to the administrative building along with many of the other travelers. The short ride into the colony was quick and relaxing. After arrival, they made their way to the in-processing section. Keyloi followed Dr. Kelba as he made his way to the counter.

He spoke with the female at the desk, showed his credentials, and asked many questions. "Andaro, we need your identification."

"Thank you, Andaro. I hope you enjoy living on Jedira," the female said.

"Thank you, Tani."

"Tani? Yes, you are from Radzier. Especially with your beautiful eyes and hair color." She cheerfully tried to engage in conversation.

"Thank you, Tani."

"I have a daughter about your age. Her name is Twilight. You may be in the same level." She gave a beautiful smile. "Speaking of your education, you will need to visit with the educational representative in the next room." She pointed toward a closed door at the end of the counter. "And Dr. Gravton, your assignment staff will be in the door just past that."

"Thank you, Tani."

"Yes, thank you," Dr. Kelba repeated. "Surely, Andaro will meet your daughter."

The female smiled again.

They moved to the educational representative's door. Keyloi registered and was informed he would begin his education in the morning. They moved to the next room to find the medical facility assignment for Dr. Gravton. Finally, they acquired a shuttle that delivered them to their unit.

Their new home was simple. Like other units, the floorplans were box-shaped with front and rear doors and a large window on each side. The structures were autogenerated as were all the buildings they had seen on the planet. It had a large common room with two doors for their resting rooms and a single door for a small relieving room. All the comforts of home.

Keyloi entered the smaller of the two sleeping rooms. He placed his belongings on the sleeper and looked around. Four bare walls, ceiling, and floor. A cube. A sleeping compartment, clothing storage built into one wall, a counter with upper and lower cabinets, and a desk chair occupied the room.

Keyloi sighed. "Hmm, comfy."

He walked back into the common room. He glanced into the doctor's room which was slightly larger than his. He looked in the small relieving room.

"Andaro, what do you think?"

"It's small but will be okay."

"This is our new home for a while. Not as nice as our home on Radzier, but we'll get adjusted to it in time."

"We will, Dad."

Dr. Kelba smiled. "Remember our last name. This is for our own good. If anyone discovers our true identities, we will be in serious trouble."

"Yes, Tani … Dad." Keyloi looked out the window and saw a few children playing in the small courtyard behind their unit. "Hustaka," the word came out before he realized it.

"Yes. We'll see if there is a team here. Why don't you ask some of your classmates tomorrow, and I'll ask around at the hospital. If there's a team, we'll find it."

Keyloi was excited about getting involved in a hustaka team and learning the sport. "Yes, that's a good idea."

"Well, let's go look around and find out where places are located. I'm ready to eat. How about you?"

"Yes, I am." He had not realized how long it had been since they had dined. He thought of how nourishment sounded good once the doctor mentioned it.

The two left the unit and began their walk. They found the Lounge where all meals were prepared daily and enjoyed their first meal on the planet. They also found the educational facility and the clinic in the hospital where the doctor's office would be. They met many humanoids enjoying the evening in groups or alone on their front stoops. The central location, called the Commons, where the colonists would gather for information and group meetings, rose in the center of a spacious undeveloped area. Simply a small octagonal pergola in the middle. Administrative, educational, medical, and other buildings surrounded the Commons. A nice peaceful area.

Jedira was quiet. The landscape lay flat with no large flora. There was grass but no trees, and the tallest of the few bushes stood waist high. As the shuttle captain stated, the vegetation had a light bluish color. Keyloi couldn't remember the name of the color the captain used and thought it an odd color for flora.

The sky grew dark. The planet's star descended. One of the satellites had already appeared in the sky, and the other peeked over the horizon. The galaxy's stars shone as the planet's star vanished. The nightscape was spectacular with twinkling stars scattered across the sky, and the satellite casting its gentle glow over the landscape.

Keyloi breathed in deeply. So quiet. The silence was loud. Nothing made a sound. No insects. No amphibians. Just the sound of humanoids as they talked and laughed. The light breeze enhanced the comfortable weather.

"It's a little too quiet tonight. I wonder if that's normal around here," the doctor commented. The sudden sound of Dr. Kelba's voice startled Keyloi. The words were loud compared to the silence around them.

"It is too quiet," Keyloi agreed as he gazed about the darkness.

"You'll get used to it," came a voice from an individual who meandered by.

The two snickered. After a little more observing and investigating, they returned to their new home and retired for the evening.

***

Keyloi opened his eyes in a hospital or clinic, he wasn't sure. He helped an adult, a doctor, to wrap another humanoid's arm. "That looks great, Keyloi," he said.

Keyloi sat up in bed and looked around at the dark, empty room. *What was that? There's the name Keyloi again. Was my name Keyloi?* After considering the dream for a few minutes, he drifted back to sleep.

Section 11

Keyloi and the doctor went to the Lounge for their morning meal. Afterward, he walked to the educational facility as instructed.

"Students, welcome Andaro Gravton. He and his father recently arrived from Radzier. Be sure to speak with him today."

He felt awkward as others stared. Only one other student in the group had a reddish tint to his skin and hair, but it paled in comparison to Keyloi's distinctive tones.

The instructor, a young female from Eden, had long blonde hair with brown highlights that struck Keyloi as attractive. He had never seen that hair color. Also, in the class, a female from Bliteque with her distinctive appearance wore a language translator to communicate. He had never personally seen anyone of that race but thought of her as very attractive. He could not keep his eyes from glancing at the two interesting-looking humanoids.

Each student took out their assigned databoards and began their work. Little interaction transpired between the students. Keyloi opened his assigned databoard to begin his work assignments. The day continued smoothly.

He met many of the other students during interaction time. He was intrigued by all the various colors of skin and hair pigments. *Is the flora on Radzier the reason that we Radzierians have red hair and skin? If that is true, then is the flora on Eden white like the instructor's hair, and purple on that girl's planet?* He pondered the truth of that statement and thought he would ask someone someday.

He spoke to a few of the youth at school, but none of them ever heard of hustaka. *They may not have a hustaka team here. I wonder what I could do to get one started. Where could we practice anyway? They may not even have a court here.*

He decided to ask Dr. Kelba about what to do. After school, he went to the unit, but the doctor was not there. He walked around the vicinity to discover the sights. He thought it interesting that everyone walked. There were very few vehicles, and those were used for transportation to the air shuttle or for security.

The modular structures used as living quarters were identical. They had the same light gray-colored surfaces with one window on each side. They were grouped in six to eight individual units in a circle facing each toward a small courtyard. These pods were placed behind the administrative, educational, medical, service, and other work-related structures, which all surrounded the Commons.

No flora existed anywhere near the units nor inside the colony. He walked to the colony edge called the Perimeter.

Plenty of flora grew outside the Perimeter. Some of the short lighter-colored blue plants had hints of greenish tones. Very odd-looking to him. He turned and ambled along the border around the colony. The entire exterior displayed the same color with few variations. He saw a few monoliths he had heard about lightly scattered throughout the landscape in small groups. Those peculiar cone-like structures rose twenty to forty feet in the air and were not large around. He wondered what they were. The star, Capria, sank to show signs of ending the day. The silhouette of one small moon could be seen. He couldn't remember its name. Nothing else occupied the sky. No clouds, no birds, not even drifting flora seeds.

He continued around the Perimeter and then turned toward the interior of the colony. He passed by several humanoids. Many greeted him cheerfully. Some talked briefly to him about nothing.

A young female his age stopped and asked, "Are you the new student at the colony?"

"Yes, we just arrived yesterday. I'm Keyloi," he said then stopped. *Keyloi? Where did that name come from?* "My name is Andaro," he corrected.

She hesitated and asked, "Andaro?"

Keyloi grinned, "Yes." He tried to hide his mistake.

She giggled. "My name is Twilight. How do you like it here so far?" she asked. Her bright blue eyes sparkled. The dark hair touched her shoulders and swayed as she spoke. Her skin had a golden glow. Keyloi stared at her beauty.

"Hello?" she asked.

Keyloi shook his head. "Oh, I'm sorry." He struggled to get the words from his mouth. "I'm not used to seeing humanoids with so many colors."

"My colors?" she giggled. "You must be from Radzier."

"I am. How did you know?" He eyed her in wonder.

"Everyone knows your planet is all red," she stated but quickly continued, "but you're red is handsome. I like your green eyes."

Keyloi blushed and averted his gaze.

She quickly changed the subject. "Have you ever visited another planet?"

"Uh, no."

"You are in for a surprise. There are lots of colors from very dark to very light at Alpha. There is someone from the other five planets here. And none of us came from Jedira," she giggled.

Keyloi thought her laughter captivating. He enjoyed listening to her talk.

"Uh," he swallowed quickly thinking of what to say, "where is your planet?

"I'm from Proxima b. My mother and I have been here for six years."

A call for Twilight came from the distance. "That's my mother. I've got to go. Maybe we can see each other tomorrow."

"Yes, I would like that," he fumbled his words.

He watched as she walked away. He realized he was breathing a little fast. *I would like that. Really? Couldn't you think of something better to say? And why did you stare at her? Why did I say Keyloi? She probably thinks I'm weird.*

Internal excitement moved him into a handspring and flip. He balanced on his hands for a minute then bounced backward onto his feet. *I think I'll like this place.*

He continued his trek along the buildings and turned toward the Lounge to get nourishment. He saw the offerings and wasn't sure if he would like them. He finally found some bread with a type of spread and a few fruits to make a simple meal. It was surprisingly better than he expected, so he got a second helping.

He watched the individuals come and go. The young Radzierian he saw at school entered with an older female who must have been his mother. Her skin and hair matched her son's.

After spending some time just observing the traffic, he decided to head back to his unit. He walked outside into a hazy glow. Capria neared its setting. He directed his steps to his unit and saw it in the distance. Dr. Kelba was standing in the doorway.

"Where have you been?" came a quiet question.

"Uh, I went for a walk and then to the Lounge." He stood outside the doorway. Dr. Kelba moved to let him inside.

"Why don't we set a schedule to meet for dinner? I enjoy dining with you, and we can share how our day was. It's kind of a family thing," the doctor suggested.

"That's a great idea," Keyloi responded. They discussed the time the doctor would be off duty each evening.

"I haven't eaten yet. You want to join me?" Dr. Kelba asked.

"Sure," Keyloi answered as they started to the Lounge.

They talked about their first day and the new experiences they encountered. They both were intrigued by the various humanoids they had met or seen.

"I never even thought I would meet a humanoid without red skin and hair," Keyloi stated in amazement.

"I know. It's very different, but I like it," the doctor responded.

"I do, too," Keyloi said with a smile as he thought of Twilight.

Section 12

Keyloi awoke before Capria rose. He gazed out the window at the spray of sparkles in the night sky. *Out there somewhere is Radzier.* He thought of recent events after arriving on planet of how nice everyone seemed to be, how he enjoyed talking with Twilight and being Dr. Kelba's son. He reflected on his life from what he remembered. That life was gone forever, but he loved his new life.

He lay for what seemed like hours and stared through his window at the night sky. He wondered if he would ever return to Radzier. Then he realized that on the entire planet he only knew Tani Dala. He wondered what Radzier would have to offer him. He was glad to be on Jedira and excited about making new friends and getting to know Twilight more.

Capria's light penetrated the sky. Keyloi got up and prepared himself for the day. After getting ready, he went to the main room and sat until his father came out of his room.

Dr. Kelba opened his door. "Good morning, Dad," Keyloi said cheerfully.

A look of surprise covered his adoptive father. "Uh, good

morning. I see you're ready to go."

"Yes, Tani," he replied.

"Good. Let me finish getting ready, and we'll leave." Soon, the doctor returned, and both left for the Lounge. Keyloi had never heard of the day's morning menu offering but found it tasty. After a relaxing breakfast, they separated toward their individual duties.

Keyloi made his way to the educational facility and waited quietly until classes began. He saw Twilight across the room, waving at him. He smiled and returned the gesture.

During their lunch break, Twilight approached him. "May I sit with you?"

Keyloi smiled. "Of course." He scooted over to give her more room.

They chatted for a few moments until classes were called. He enjoyed having a new friend, especially her as his new friend.

The days passed smoothly. He felt more comfortable about being around the other students. He enjoyed their company and friendship. Daily, as soon as classes were released, he would meet with his friends for various activities. He asked if they were interested in learning hustaka. Mostly curiosity was returned.

One evening, the doctor said, "I've been thinking, why don't you start coming to my clinic after classes? You can help me in the afternoon. You can learn basic medical and will probably impress everyone there. And I need an assistant."

Keyloi thought he may like being around the hospital

environment, so the next day, he arrived at the clinic where he was introduced to a few members as well as the location of basic items. He retrieved things for Dr. Kelba and assisted with small injuries. He enjoyed his new practical education.

Daily, he sat with Twilight and other students for lunch and gained friends. He couldn't join them for too long after school. He replied that his dad needed him at the clinic. He wanted to take part in their social events but was torn between his work education and friends. Many times, Dr. Kelba would release Keyloi from his responsibility early so he could enjoy his friends.

One day, his father came home late without speaking his words properly. He wasn't his usual self. Keyloi wondered what happened to him, so he asked if everything was okay.

"I'm fine," came the slurred answer.

Keyloi hesitated, "Can I do anything for you?"

"I said I'm fine," he responded loudly and closed his eyes.

Keyloi paused for a moment, then asked, "I'm going to the Lounge. Would you like me to bring you anything?"

"Not tonight," he fumbled his words. "I'm going to rest."

Keyloi stared at him. He had never seen him act like that before. He wandered to the Lounge alone, wondering why his father acted so differently. *Maybe something happened after I left the clinic. I hope he gets some good rest and tomorrow will be better for him.* He was deeply concerned.

As he finished his meal, a couple of his new friends entered. They sat and talked for a while until they realized how late it had become. After farewells, Keyloi returned to his unit and bed. He lay quietly for a few moments, gazing out the window at the beautiful nightscape. Soon, he rested.

***

He awakened. No noise, no touch, no light, just a sense pricked his thoughts. He opened his eyes and, in the darkness, saw his door open. He typically closed his door, but it wasn't important enough to get up, so he returned to his peaceful sleep.

As time went on, he found his door open regularly. He thought that either he forgot to close it, or the door latch broke. It did not concern him since he was safe and always slept peacefully.

***

Weeks and months progressed wonderfully. Keyloi gained friends, did well in his studies, and increased his learning at his father's clinic. He found his voice deepened and noticed that his muscles were getting larger. He enjoyed the school's physical activities program and exceled in all he tried. He found no hustaka sport on planet but learned and practiced the moves himself. He made many friends at school. His friendship with Twilight grew as well as his relationship with his father. He and his dad shared numerous fun times together as well as their inmost feelings. He was happy.

Occasionally, Dr. Kelba came home not his normal happy

self. Keyloi wondered what happened. Why had his personality changed? He thought something might be going on at the hospital. Keyloi asked him about his work, but the doctor always said all was fine.

Keyloi touched his dad's arm and said, "If I can help any way, just tell me what I can do." His heart went out to him.

Dr. Kelba looked at Keyloi's hand on his arm for a moment. "I'll be okay."

"Okay. I love you, Dad," he sincerely responded. "Maybe you need to get some rest. You do work long hours sometimes."

The doctor sighed and looked into Keyloi's eyes. After a few moments, he responded, "I'm sure you're right. I'll go ahead and go to bed. I love you, too, Son." He got up and went directly into his bedroom.

Keyloi was worried about his dad's change in behavior. He seemed distracted and not in his normal frame of mind. He went to his bedroom and prepared for a night's rest. As he lay looking out his window, he wished he could help his dad somehow.

***

Keyloi felt something touch his arm. He opened his eyes to see his father sitting on the side of his bed. His hand touched Keyloi's shoulder. The surprised youth drew back.

The sudden awakening befuddled Keyloi. "Dad?"

"It's okay, Andaro," said the doctor. "I've been thinking about us being a family. We've been creating family traditions, customs, and relationships. We've gotten closer since moving here, and I wanted to share a family custom with you."

"Of course, Dad, but what are you talking about?" Keyloi didn't understand why he acted the way he did.

"I love you, Andaro," the doctor said as he gently rubbed the boy's shoulder. "I want us to be a closer family than we are now and to love each other like all families do." He put his hand on the side of the youth's face.

"Dad?" Keyloi was confused.

"Families take care of each other and protect each other. Sometimes families show their love to each other that they don't share with anyone else. Do you understand?" The doctor put his right hand on Keyloi's chest. "Don't be afraid. I won't hurt you."

Keyloi's voice cracked, "Tani?" Fear gripped the boy as the doctor's hand slid to his stomach. He raised his knee, knocking the man's hand away. He rolled off the sleeper away from his adoptive father. He landed on his hands and knees and quickly gained composure.

"Andaro, stop," came a harsh demand.

"I don't want you touching me like that," Keyloi announced as his heart raced and breathing amplified.

"I'm not going to hurt you. I want to teach you some new things."

"I don't want to learn anything like that." He moved toward the door.

Dr. Kelba grasped his forearm. "Come back here."

Keyloi twisted his arm to gain relief from the grasp. Dr. Kelba stood.

"Leave me alone," the boy demanded.

"Why are you treating me like this? I only want the best for you," the man held his hand out toward the youth.

Keyloi continued toward the door but felt another grasp on his arm. Using his hustaka instinct, his left foot shot up into the man's underarm, knocking away the grip. Dr. Kelba advanced. Keyloi's other foot fluently glided as a swinging weapon that connected with the adult's chest. The man was knocked off balance.

"Andaro! Will you stop it?" he roared his demand.

Keyloi headed out the doorway and through the front door. While running, he heard his adoptive father yell his name. He continued running. Tears blurred his vision as the resulting emotions exploded. He used the back of his hands to clear the moisture. He stopped at the Perimeter and glanced around the area. Bracing himself against a building, Keyloi allowed the tears to freely flow. He dropped to his knees in anguish with the feeling of embarrassment.

I trusted him. Why would he do that? Hyperventilating, he attempted to gain control of his feelings. *His hands covered his face in shame.*

"Andaro?" came a distant call. Keyloi raised his face toward to sound. He looked around for a hiding place. He glanced outside the Perimeter. *I can't do that.* He searched toward some of the structures opposite the calling. He ran.

Soon, he noticed an angle in the design of the educational facility that was in the shadows. He crawled into the crook and grew silent. He listened. He heard his heartbeat; his silent breathing disturbed the stillness.

"Andaro?" came a loud whisper.

Keyloi refused to move. He saw an image fifteen meters away to his right slowly pass behind a structure. He closed his eyes.

"Andaro, come back home. I won't hurt you."

Keyloi remained still. The individual soon left the area. The boy relaxed.

Section 13

Keyloi sat up. The nightmare he experienced was fresh in his mind. Fear enveloped him. He leaned his back against the building. His sleepwear was wet from the night mists. He didn't want to do anything. He couldn't think of the day. His mind hurt. His energy was depleted.

Devoid of a timepiece, he peeked around the corner to see numerous colonists ambling toward their duties. He knew colony operations would be starting soon. Fresh clothing and breakfast were his desires, but he wanted to avoid his adoptive father. Retreating around the corner of the building, he rested out of sight. With hunger and the need to freshen up, he would wait until after Dr. Kelba left for the Lounge or the clinic, then he would make his rounds and end up in his classes.

After traffic slowed, he stealthily made his way to his unit and crept inside. Quietly, he went to each room and discovered the unit was empty. Relief enveloped him. He quickly cleaned up and left for the Lounge.

Upon entering, he noticed two tables occupied. No doctor

in sight. He stepped inside and found what he wanted for breakfast. He gathered his food and upon turning to leave, he came face to face with Dr. Kelba. Keyloi froze. He almost dropped his nourishment.

His adoptive father walked toward him. Keyloi cowered back. The adult towered directly over his son and whispered, "Don't be afraid of me. I won't hurt you. About last night, you can't tell anyone. First, it's a family secret, and no one else should know what we do. Second, if you go to the authorities, they will discover who you are and will hand you over to those looking for you. And they won't like how you treat me by telling family things to others. Finally, I have already discovered one humanoid in this colony who is searching for you. You need to be careful who you talk to, or you will end up with them. Do you understand me?" The doctor spoke firmly but in a pleading manner.

A quiet response came, "Yes, Tani." Keyloi did not take his eyes off his father.

"Come on, Andaro. I only want the best for both of us."

Keyloi stared at the adult.

"You need to get to your classes."

"Yes, Tani."

Keyloi made his way to the educational facility and tried not to look back. His instincts told him Dr. Kelba was gone, but he still had suspicions.

As had been usual, Twilight waited on him.

"Hey, Andaro," came the cheerful greeting.

He quietly returned her greeting.

After a small hesitation, she asked, "Are you okay?"

He looked away. "I'm fine."

"You must have had a bad night. You look terrible." She looked concerned.

"Yeah, it was bad."

"Maybe it will get better as the day goes on." Her cheerful positiveness would have been unwanted, but he welcomed whatever Twilight said.

The day did not get any better. Keyloi couldn't get his mind off the terror and onto his studies. No matter what he did, his mind drifted back into his escape. He found strength in the way he reacted with hustaka moves. He didn't have to think about it because it felt spontaneous.

Before he realized it, classes were dismissed for the day. He slowly made his way to his unit. Inside, he went to his room and sat on the floor in the corner. He covered his head with his blanket. His mind replayed all the visions of horror he had experienced. He cried softly.

He heard the exterior door open and his name being called. He sat quietly. His door opened, and the doctor asked why he hadn't responded.

Keyloi didn't move. He heard the adult make his way into the room. His nerves stood on end. He heard the doctor sit on the floor beside him.

"Andaro," he paused. "Andaro, look at me," he said sternly.

The youth slowly lowered the blanket from his head. His tear-stained eyes peered at his abuser. He trembled.

"Look, I'm sorry if you feel bad. I never wanted that. We are all we have, and we need each other. All this is a new experience for you. I thought you were old enough to share my love. I want to take care of you and be your father. Tomorrow, come to the clinic after classes. You can help around the clinic. How about that?"

Keyloi lowered his head. He barely heard the words.

After a minute of silence, the doctor said, "Well, you rest well tonight." At that he got up and walked out of the room.

Keyloi covered his head again. He sat for a little longer and finally got into his sleeper. He left on his outer clothes and wrapped his blanket tightly around him. He felt vulnerable.

***

Capria's light broke the darkness of night. Keyloi got up and prepared himself for the day. He went to the main room and waited.

The doctor's door opened, and he was visibly surprised to see Keyloi waiting on him. "Glad to see you up," came a warm greeting.

Keyloi didn't respond. They left for breakfast. Dr. Kelba said he will see him after classes at the clinic to help him learn his new responsibility. Again, the youth did not respond.

"Did you hear me?"

"Yes, Tani," he slowly answered.

Keyloi walked toward his classes. As he drew near, he decided not to go that day. He walked toward the building but turned just as he arrived. He wasn't sure if the doctor was watching him or not. He walked to the rear of the building and found a door unlocked. It was a cleaning closet with a connecting door into the school's main hallway. He closed both doors, sat on an upturned bucket, and leaned against a wall. He didn't want to be at school. He didn't want to be on Jedira. He didn't want to be near the doctor. Everything seemed totally hopeless.

He sat for about an hour when the door to the hallway opened.

"Well, what do we have here?" a pleasant female voice sounded.

Keyloi was startled and looked up. His tear-stained eyes were exposed. His sad, depressing appearance brought the female into the room. She closed the door.

"What's going on, Young One?" She knelt in front of him. Her face glowed like a radiant beam into his soul. Her deep blue eyes and weathered complexion invited emotions. He lowered his head.

"Do you want to talk about something?" Kindness surrounded her every word.

Keyloi didn't respond.

"Well,"— she began as she sat on the floor in front of

him— "Miss Myla doesn't want any young lad around her to be down and out. There's too much good in life to be sad."

Keyloi couldn't stop a tear from trickling down his face. He quickly wiped it off.

Miss Myla handed him a clean towel from a rack behind her. "Here you go. You take care of that handsome face, and then maybe we can find out what happened to make you so sad."

Keyloi wiped his face. *I can't tell her what happened. Dr. Kelba will turn me over to those humanoids who are after me.* He shook his head.

"Well, if you don't want to talk to me, is there anyone you would like to talk with?"

He repeated the action.

"So, are you going to stay in here all day?"

No response.

"Whatever is bothering you is huge, isn't it? You don't know of any way out of it, do you?" Her words were kind.

Keyloi slowly raised his eyes to her.

"Sometimes we have issues with someone or some situation, and we can't find an answer. If you can, just believe that the future is going to be better for you. No matter what happens now, be optimistic and expect things to change for your best. Someone is always watching over us for our good. Work for a better tomorrow, and your future will be wonderful."

Keyloi stared at her. He didn't know how to respond. He didn't hear what she said but how she said it was comforting. Her voice drew him into her like water to a dry mouth.

"Listen, you sit here as long as you need. I'll be back from time to time and"—she lowered her voice—"I won't tell anyone you're in here."

He continued to stare at her. She picked up a few items and walked out into the hallway. He watched her quietly close the door.

Keyloi sat in silence for hours. His mind wandered to a hundred topics. He hated feeling like that. He hated being there. He hated the doctor. He hated himself. He felt dirty. Ashamed. Tears flowed once again.

After a while, Miss Myla returned. "Hello again, little fellow. I wondered if you would still be here. I brought something for you to snack on. Troubles are hard on the body, and you need to eat something tasty." She pulled up a small bucket, turned it upside down next to him, and placed a container of small berries on top. He stared at it.

"Haven't you had katerfruit? They're a tasty treat." Her voice was too cheerful for him. "She turned up another bucket and made a small seat for herself. "Now, is there anything else I can help you with?"

Keyloi turned his head.

"I guess not right now. You understand that this room is available for you at any time. Got it?" She ducked her head and looked up into his eyes.

He raised his eyes to see hers. He nodded.

"Maybe I'll see you again, but remember, I'm always here." At that, she smiled and exited the room.

Keyloi sat for a short while longer. He wondered if classes would be over soon. He peeked into the hallway and saw no one. He closed that door and opened the outside door. He could see some youth milling around the Commons. He started toward the hospital clinic. He didn't want to be turned over to some humanoids. He wondered what they would do to him. He entered the clinic and went to Dr. Kelba's office.

"There you are. How was school?"

Keyloi didn't know how to answer him. He lowered his head.

"Okay. Follow me, and I'll show you what to do." His training on new procedures contained no problems. Dr. Kelba eased close to him when he was explaining something in detail. It unnerved Keyloi.

After the day ended, they went directly to the Lounge. Keyloi had a small meal. He wasn't very hungry. They sat quietly, and the doctor spoke occasionally. When they went to their unit, Keyloi went to his room and closed his door. He got into his sleeper and wrapped his blanket around himself. He stared out the window. His mind reflected on what the lady in the closet said. He couldn't remember her name or the details. *Why didn't I listen better?*

Section 14

The next day arrived and Keyloi quickly got up and waited for the doctor. He returned to the closet retreat.

Miss Myla arrived again. "I see you're back. Are you any better today?"

Keyloi quietly answered, "Yes, Tani." He thought of how he could physically embrace her words as they left her mouth. He just looked at her hoping that she would just speak.

"Oh, you must be from Radzier. I love that crimson planet."

Keyloi smiled.

"Now, there's that handsome smile that I hoped to see." She smiled.

He lowered his head.

She pulled up her overturned bucket and sat facing him. "Young one, listen to me for a minute." She took his hands in hers. He hesitated but didn't feel uneasy about her warm hands holding his. "You can't just sit in this room all day during school. As much as I wouldn't mind you staying right there, your responsibility is to your education. I want you to be some great well-known humanoid when you grow up, but you need your education to prepare for it." Her loving eyes pierced through his very soul.

"Yes, Tani," he slowly replied.

"So, what about getting to your class?" She lightly slapped his knee twice.

"Yes, Tani." He knew he needed to go to his classes. He knew that sitting in that cleaning room all day would help nothing. He slowly got up. She opened the door and escorted him out.

"I'll see you later, and when you're ready to talk, Miss Myla is right here."

Keyloi smiled faintly as he exited the room. He headed down the hallway to his class, which was already in session. He walked in as the entire class looked at him.

"Andaro Gravton," the instructor spoke. "You must know that we do not tolerate missing your education. Be seated and begin your work. We will talk later." The instructor was not the regular female he loved to see. This male was tall and thin with a large head. He had light skin and supplemented his speaking with his hands. He spoke in directives rather than instructing tones.

Keyloi moved to his assigned desk and opened his databoard to where he had stopped. He waited until the instructor's eyes were off him, then he looked over at Twilight. She looked at the instructor and then back to him.

"Are you okay?" she mouthed.

He shook his head with no facial expression, then turned back to his studies.

The morning progressed, but his thoughts often reflected on the terror. He completed his learning section and moved into the next.

During lunch, Twilight found him.

"Okay, you need to talk to me," she said quietly but sternly.

"What about?" he answered knowing what she wanted.

"What happened to you? Where were you yesterday? You are the boy I enjoy hanging around with most of all, but one day you are suddenly not yourself. What's going on?"

He looked at his meal and didn't reply. *I would never tell her what Dr. Kelba did. I won't tell anyone. He said it was my fault, but what did I do? I feel ashamed of what happened. If I told her, she wouldn't want to talk to me.* He looked around the room at the dozens of students having their lunch. He saw two males and one female at different tables looking at him. He quickly looked away. *They already know about it. What are they thinking about me?*

"Andaro?" came a quiet inquiry. "Are you okay?"

He turned and looked at Twilight. "I don't know."

"Did something happen to you? You're not acting yourself." Her words were drowned in concern.

He straightened his back and looked toward the ceiling.

He exhaled. He paused and said, "I'm fine. I'll be okay."

"I hope the real Andaro returns soon. I miss him," she said as she took a bite of her meal.

He looked down at her plate and paused. "I do, too," he said quietly.

After a few minutes, two other students came to their table. They greeted Keyloi and asked where he was the day before.

He paused. "Hiding."

They looked at him with smiles. "From whom?" one of the males jested.

He paused again. "Everyone."

They all laughed and made comments about how they want to hide sometimes, who they would hide from, and where they could go to hide. Keyloi saw that they were just having fun without acknowledging his pain. He felt that was good so they wouldn't pry for answers.

"Did you hear about the groundquakes?" a male joined the group. Two females followed him to the discussion.

"I didn't know the planet had those," another commended.

"Yes, I heard they are so big that the ground explodes," the first added.

The others had mixed responses of disbelief and surprise.

"My father is a planetary geologist and said that there are no records of them happening on Jedira. I think they sent the

Scouts out to investigate," he explained.

"I met a Scout once. He was so brave and handsome," a female reminisced as she gazed at the ceiling. The others laughed.

"I'm going to be a Scout when I get older. I want to explore the multiverse," Broban envisioned.

"We lived by a teenager who left for the Scout Academy a few years ago. He must have come back to visit his family because I saw him at his parents' unit last week," the female explained. "He's so handsome in his uniform."

"I'm definitely joining," Broban added with a smile. The girl smiled at him. The others awed at them.

The conversation continued until classes were called. The remainder of the day was as usual. Keyloi felt accepted again but still felt a fear the others would find out, and he would be rejected.

After classes ended, Keyloi made his way to the clinic. He stood outside the clinic door and took a deep breath and then exhaled. He finally opened the door and entered to see the doctor reviewing his databoard.

"How did your day go?"

Keyloi hesitated, "It went well."

"Where were you yesterday? Your instructor told me you weren't at class and that you were late today."

He didn't know how to answer.

"Andaro," the doctor started, "answer me."

"I, uh…" He was shocked by the doctor knowing he missed classes.

"Yes?" he strongly articulated.

Keyloi searched for an answer. He trembled inside. He stuttered again. "I, uh, was, uh…" He froze. Dr. Kelba shifted toward him. Keyloi ran out of the clinic.

"Andaro?" he called. "Okay. I'll see you at home." Keyloi overheard him comment to himself.

Keyloi ran. He didn't know where he wanted to go, but he just ran. He went behind buildings and between some more. He headed for the Perimeter. He stopped. He had never gone past the Perimeter boundary. He just stared into the open space. Nothing but small flora for kilometers. He whimpered. *What am I going to do now? I don't want to be caught. What can I do?* He fell on his knees and cried. Loneliness, sorrow, pain, fear, hopelessness. Emotions swirled through him in a tidal wave of agony.

After a couple of hours in distress, he reasoned what he should do. *If I run away, there is nowhere to go, and I can't survive out there by myself. If I don't go home, he will find me and give me to those searching for me. If I do go home, he will hurt me again. If I am nice to him and obey him, maybe he won't hurt me.* He rationalized his actions and decided to be the best son he could be. That would give him less pain.

He got to his feet, wiped his eyes and started back to the unit. As he was nearing the building, he looked for the doctor. He grasped the handle and slowly opened the door. He looked around and entered. He went directly to his room, entered, and closed the door.

"Andaro?"

Fear melted over Keyloi's entire body. He quickly turned to see the doctor sitting in the desk chair. He backed away.

Dr. Kelba stood up and walked to the lad.

Keyloi stammered, "I went for a walk."

"I told you I don't want to hurt you. Why are you so afraid of me?" he questioned as he stepped toward the youth.

Keyloi backed up. His breath was heavy and quivering. His heart pounded.

"I only wanted to show you how much I care for you."

In a quivering voice, Keyloi replied, "I've never heard of any family doing that."

"It's because they don't talk about it. You are growing up and soon will be an adult. I'm trying to teach you as you grow."

Keyloi said nothing.

"Trust me, Andaro," the doctor said, "I only want the best for you and me."

The doctor left the room and Keyloi got into his sleeper. He closed his eyes but couldn't sleep. He lay still looking out the window into the dark sky. He trembled. Tears slowly ran down his cheeks. He couldn't think. He didn't want to. He took in a big breath, closed his eyes, and slowly exhaled. He knew this couldn't be normal in a family.

***

He saw a Pulodian, a creature from the southern hemisphere from Radzier. It was very tall with four arms, four eyes, and a large head. It glared at him and Keyloi knew it wanted to eat him. He ran, but the beast followed and wrapped his arms around him. As he screamed, he awoke. Keyloi's heart pounded, his blanket was wet with sweat, and he hyperventilated. He realized it was a dream. He sat up and rubbed his face. After a few minutes, he inhaled deeply and returned to his sleeper. After a short while, he slept again.

***

The Pulodian was in front of him. Keyloi screamed and tried to fight it away, but it was much larger and stronger than he. He awoke. He was frustrated with those nightmares. Soon, he returned to sleep.

***

The same creature appeared. He was holding Keyloi's arm and pulling him into his bosom. The creature's mouth opened, and he felt a piercing pain in his forearm. He awoke with a gasp.

Keyloi lay and stared into the darkness wiping his eyes. *I am not going to let this get me. I will fight you, and I will win.* He became angry at the doctor and was ready to take whatever steps needed to fix his situation. He finally rested.

***

The creature reappeared behind him. Anger rose up in Keyloi, and he turned to face the giant. "Stop it." The monster advanced. Keyloi sprung high and kicked the creature's face. It stumbled but resumed its approach. He sprung feet first toward the being, impacting its legs. The giant crumbled. Keyloi stood, crossed his arms, and shouted, "No more!" The monster froze with a confused look on its face. Keyloi awoke and felt empowered to take control. He closed his eyes again and rested.

***

The lady in the kitchen stood before him. They were surrounded by a canopy of the forest. She held out her hand and said, "It's going to be okay, Keyloi." He took her hand and experienced a peace he hadn't felt in a while. "Keyloi," came the name from beside her from a man in a doctor's coat. Kindness was on his face. He awoke peacefully.

Who are those people? Are they my real parents? Is my name Keyloi? He pondered on his visions but came to no conclusion. He knew Capria would be rising soon, so he got up and sat in his chair.

Section 15

As Capria's light brightened his room, Keyloi rose and prepared himself for the day.

"Good morning," the doctor said.

Keyloi glanced at him then looked at the floor.

"Let's go," he said as he moved toward the door. They walked toward the Lounge. He breathed in a stale odor that was faint but distinct.

Keyloi ate what he could, but his emotions made it hard for him to think clearly. He drank a couple of servings of fruit juices and nibbled on soft foods. Finally, they left and departed ways.

He sat through classes, trying to keep his mind off the situation and on the topics. During lunch, Twilight asked why he was so different lately. He was ashamed to tell her.

"I'm just not feeling well lately," he finally said.

"Your father is a doctor, go see him," she said matter-of-factly.

Keyloi didn't answer. There was no need. He couldn't explain it to her anyway without explaining what happened.

Broban came to the table. "Did you guys hear about the caprodomes eating humanoids?"

"What?" the others responded in unison.

"That's what I heard in the south."

"They're not eating anyone." Another boy arrived to give clarity. "They are scoping out the area."

"Wait," Keyloi was confused. "What's a caprodome?"

"They are monsters that live on the planet. They sit on top of the monoliths and watch for something to feed their babies," one boy answered excitedly.

"There are no such things as caprodomes," Twilight said.

Classes were called to start.

Broban replied as they all got up from the table. "Yes, there are. I heard someone took a photo of one."

"Whatever," Twilight responded in disbelief as the group split up.

Classes resumed. His studies could not distract him. His mind continually returned to shame and guilt. He felt as though everyone was looking at him. He glanced at the timepiece and was glad classes would be over in a few minutes. He straightened up his desk area in preparation for leaving.

The day ended, and he left the room without speaking to anyone. He directed his steps to the clinic. Upon arriving, he found a new assistant talking with Dr. Kelba. Keyloi stood at the door and waited. The male glanced toward him as he spoke with the doctor.

"Can we help you?" the young adult asked.

Dr. Kelba answered, "This is my son, Andaro. He's here for training."

"Oh, that's wonderful. It's always good to have adolescents helping in the hospital. Do you have a responsibility yet?" He directed his question toward Keyloi.

The doctor answered, "Yes, he does. He's helping me as my assistant. He'll be a fine doctor one day." His dad's words were convincing.

Just then a groundquake happened. The windows shook and items fell from their shelves. It stopped as quickly as it began.

"What was that?" Keyloi asked.

The intern looked out the windows to see all was normal. "Another groundquake?

The door opened. "Is everyone okay?" asked a young female.

"Yes, we are well," the intern answered. She left as quickly as she entered.

"Very well. If that's all you have for me, I'll carry on," the male said.

"That's all, thank you." He left the room. Dr. Kelba turned to his son, "I have two things for you today, and then you can leave. I will be there a little later tonight." He turned back to his databoard.

"Yes, Tani," Keyloi responded. He started his

assignments. One was to conduct an inventory of the units of dologra, which was a pain eliminator. The other was to clean the breakroom. Those were simple tasks, and when he finished, he left for the unit.

As he was crossing the Commons, he felt he needed to stretch his muscles, so he did preliminary stretches and then conducted some hustaka moves. He ran and performed a double handspring with a flip in the air. He landed on his feet. He was proud of being able to do that. He wanted to learn even more routines.

Broban ran to him exclaiming how amazing that was. He wanted to see it again and to learn how to do it. Keyloi quickly sampled some simple hustaka moves he had learned. Broban tried to do the same, but Keyloi saw he needed assistance.

They talked for a short while when two other classmates arrived. Soon, there were eight youth in the Commons trying to do handstands and somersaults. Keyloi loved the group participation and dreamed of having a hustaka team on Jedira. Time got away from him, and when he realized he needed to go home, he told the others that he had to leave. He quickly ran toward his unit.

He arrived out of breath. He hadn't exercised like that in a few days. He opened the door to see Dr. Kelba sitting in the main room looking at him.

"I'm sorry I wasn't here when you arrived. Some students saw me doing hustaka and wanted to learn how to do it. Can I help start a team here?"

"I don't know. Maybe. Come on in," a stern response accompanied a slur in his words surprised Keyloi.

Keyloi entered and closed the door. "Are you okay? You're not speaking your words correctly. Do you need to get some rest?"

The doctor got up and grabbed Keyloi's arm.

"Dad?"

"Get in your room." He shoved him across the room toward his door.

"Stop, please," he pleaded.

Keyloi ran into his room and closed the door and held it tightly. The doctor came to the door and easily pushed it open. Anger flared from the doctor's eyes at the innocent youth. He slammed the door.

"You just can't learn, can you?" The doctor closed in.

"What are you talking about?" Keyloi asked in surprise.

The back of the adult's hand impacted the youth's right cheek. Keyloi screamed, grabbed his cheek, and crouched down in the corner. He was shocked at the impact. After two more blows, the doctor grabbed his adopted son's arm.

"You need to stop treating me this way."

Keyloi cowered in fear. He cried. Dr. Kelba slapped him.

"Stop it," the doctor demanded.

Keyloi pushed the doctor as hard as he could and ran for the door. The adult fell to the floor and scrambled to get up.

Keyloi opened the door and ran.

Section 16

Keyloi ran to the school's closet hoping it was unlocked. It was and he entered and locked the door. His hand, arm, and face hurt, but his heart ached severely. He trembled inside. He couldn't move. Tears flooded his already tear-stained cheeks. He couldn't think; he didn't want to.

I'm going to fix this somehow. I'm tired of him treating me this way. I'm tired of his blaming me for things that are not my fault. I'm not going to let him keep pushing me around like he has. I need a plan to get out of here. Where would I go? Maybe Twilight's family would let me stay there until I could go… He stopped. Where would he go? He knew no one in the multiverse but only the ones he met on Jedira. *I'll think of something.* With that determination, he stopped thinking about anything. He gathered four clean towels and made a small bed. He made himself as comfortable as he could and tried to rest.

***

The next morning, Keyloi waited before going to the Lounge. He didn't want to encounter Dr. Kelba. He arrived to find a couple of his classmates dining with their families. He asked if he could join them. They accepted, and he enjoyed his time without the doctor.

He was about to leave when Dr. Kelba entered.

"Where were you last night?" the doctor whispered to him.

"I don't want to be around you," Keyloi spoke matter-of-factly.

"Andaro?" The doctor made a shocking face.

"I'm not your son. My name is Keyloi," he whispered sternly in return. He felt taking on the new name he kept hearing in his dreams would separate him from the doctor.

His adoptive father just stood there, gaping as Keyloi passed by him. "Where did you hear that name?"

"It's my name, and I know it," he stated.

"I'm turning you over to those humanoids today," the doctor threatened.

"That will be good. I'm sure they will not treat me the way you do." He responded as he left.

Keyloi walked to the Perimeter and gazed across the early morning scenery. He allowed the internal heat of the conversation to cool off. Drops of mist covered everything. Soon, he made his way to the educational facility and found Twilight.

"Hey Twilight," he greeted cheerfully.

"Well, are you back to your regular self?" she asked.

"I hope so, and I plan on staying that way. Can you help me with something?"

"I'll try."

"I need a place to stay. Can I stay at your unit, or do you know anywhere I could go?"

Visibly, Twilight was caught unaware. She hesitated and stammered a bit. "Why can't you stay at your unit with your dad?"

Keyloi paused. *Are you really going to tell her about him?* He swallowed.

Classes were called to begin.

"We'll talk later."

"Okay, Andaro. Maybe at lunch?" she questioned raising her eyebrows.

"Uh, yes, at lunch."

Class began as usual. Keyloi got involved in his studies but occasionally drifted into the thoughts of what he planned to do. He was determined to get away from Dr. Kelba but didn't know how that would happen. *Everyone thinks he is so wonderful. They don't know him like I do.*

The morning crept along. He wanted to finish his conversation with Twilight. Soon, they were sitting together at lunch, and he was about to explain when two students came to sit with them. He mouthed the words 'later' to her. She nodded.

"Did you hear that rumble this morning before Capria rose? I wonder if it was another groundquake?" one student asked.

"Yes, and there was one after classes yesterday," another

spoke up.

"I felt that one," a third student said.

Two more youth joined them. One piped in, "I heard there was a big one south of here."

"What was that odor outside this morning? Did anyone notice that?" another asked.

"I did. Do you know what it was?" Keyloi asked.

"No, I hadn't smelled it this strong before," the male said.

"I haven't either. You remember they are expanding the colony in the south. Maybe that's what is going on," another male stated.

They continued talking even though no one had an answer.

A female student joined them and asked if they heard about everyone leaving the planet. The group was in disbelief at her words.

"No, really. My father overheard two Scouts discussing how difficult it would be when the entire planet was evacuated," she explained. "He didn't hear them say why that would happen."

More discussion began on the matter. Thoughts of what could happen and where everyone would go took over the conversation. Classes were called, so the group broke up to their assigned areas.

After classes, Keyloi met with Twilight.

"What were you wanting to talk about? You need a place

to stay?" she asked.

"Twilight, the doctor is not my father. No one knows that. My family was killed in a landslide on Radzier. He said his family was killed, too. Dr. Kelba is his real name. He adopted me and brought me here. Andaro is not my name; I think my real name is Keyloi. I remember very little about my past. He treats me badly and threatens to turn me over to some humanoids who are searching for me."

Twilight was visibly stunned. "Have you talked to the authorities?"

"He said they are looking for me, too."

The female stared at him. "Andaro, what are you saying? Why is someone looking for you?"

"I don't know, and my name is not Andaro. That's just a name I chose, because no one knew my real name," he explained.

She hesitated. "What are you going to do?"

"I don't know, but I can't go back there with him. He will beat me again and ..." he stopped. He couldn't divulge the horror that could have been done to him. He felt a tear developing so he looked away.

"I don't know if you can live with us. The colony is not that large, and he will find you. Your father is well liked as a medical doctor, so people may not believe what you're saying."

"He's not my real father, I keep telling you," Keyloi tried to explain.

"Let me talk to my mother and see what she can do,"

Twilight looked confused at how to answer.

"Can I go talk to her with you?"

"Uh," she hesitated, "let me talk to her first, and then we'll see what she says," she said. "I'll talk with you later."

Keyloi watched her walk away. He was baffled. He thought if anyone could help him, she would. Doesn't anyone care about him? He couldn't go back to the unit, so he would go back to the closet for the night.

After classes, he stealthily went to the Lounge for dinner alone. He knew if the doctor arrived while he was there, he would not make a scene in front of anyone else. With that thought, he felt safe.

After he ate, he walked around the Perimeter until dusk. He decided to go to the closet to make sure it was unlocked. He kept an eye out for the doctor. What would he do if he encountered his father, especially behind some buildings or away from everyone else? He determined not to allow himself to get caught in corners where there was no escape.

The closet was unlocked, so he entered and turned on the light. He locked the exterior door and made sure the door into the hallway was locked as well. He found some towels on a shelf to use as his pillow. He had nothing to cover. He missed his comfortable sleeper. He turned off the lights, and, in the absolute darkness, he felt where he planned to sleep. He lay down and stretched out on the floor. Soon he was resting.

Section 17

He awoke to a dark room. He wished he had a power light. He searched around with his hands for the exterior door and slowly opened it. He could see that Capria was just beginning to rise. *Perfect timing.*

He got up and went into the hallway to the relieving room. Water felt good on his morning face. He tidied himself up to not arouse suspicion that he had been there all night and then left for the Lounge. Breakfast was quick and simple so he could leave before the doctor arrived. He went to where the students gathered before classes and waited.

It felt like a groundquake occurred. *What is going on? Those are happening all the time now. I wonder if the colony is going to be evacuated like the others heard. Maybe some of the students will have more information today.*

The students began to fill up the area. Finally, Twilight arrived and sat beside Keyloi.

"Hey, Twilight, did you talk with your mother?"

She paused. "Yes, I mentioned it, but she likes your father, or whoever he is, and doesn't believe he would be bad."

Keyloi lowered his head.

"I'm sorry, but I don't know what to do. Have you thought about going to a security guard or the Scouts?"

"They won't believe me either. Who would believe a twelve-year-old against an *upstanding doctor*." Keyloi exaggerated when he used that description of his adoptive father.

Broban quickly came up to them and asked, "Have you heard that the colony is evacuating?"

"What?" the two exclaimed together.

"Yes, my mother heard that from one of the colony administrators. They started the evacuation today. The colonists from the other colonies are leaving now. I hear the south and west of Alpha are being attacked."

"Attacked by what?" Keyloi asked.

"I don't know. I hope we can get out before it comes here," Broban replied.

"What does that mean? Why are we still going to classes if that is true?" Twilight asked.

Another male came up and asked, "Have you heard about the evacuation?"

"We just have," Keyloi answered.

"It's true. We will dismiss early today to get ready to go. They are posting a notice this morning with times for us to leave."

"Just like that, we are leaving. No explanation?" Twilight asked.

"Maybe? If an evacuation is urgent, they don't give too many details," Broban replied.

The various conversation topics about evacuation circled the classes. During the first class, the students were told that an evacuation had begun with the southern and western colonists. Other colonies were arriving for their flights off the planet.

As classes began, the announcement was made. "Classes will be canceled at noon today, and you must take all your belongings with you out of this building. Evacuation means gathering as much as possible, so nothing is left behind but the structures. Your classes will be given tasks to complete in preparation for leaving. No one is allowed to leave until you are officially released."

This may be a good time to get away from the doctor. I'll keep looking for a chance. Keyloi's mind raced to new plans.

The day passed, with everything different. Keyloi's class was assigned to the cafeteria along with another class. They removed food packages, utensils, and numerous food replicators. Then they were instructed to clean out their personal lockers.

The educational facility was cleaned and stripped of everything by the end of the morning. The students were all released with tears of the possibility of never seeing each other again.

"Goodbye, Andaro, or Keyloi. I hope things work out for your best." Concern was in Twilight's voice.

"Goodbye, Twilight. Maybe we will see each other again

soon," he said.

They both watched as one of the air shuttles hovered above the portal, discharged their engines, and ascended until they left the atmosphere.

Twilight hugged Keyloi and walked away. He watched her depart, until she slipped around a unit. *Now, what? I need to stay away from the doctor, but when will I be able to leave?*

He walked through the Commons and watched the numerous colonists busy with their preparations. He saw ground shuttles of colonists he assumed were from other colonies. He thought he would go to the air portal and see if there was a schedule for him to leave. He walked in that direction but noticed a huge group of colonists in and around the air portal.

He stood in line for almost an hour. When he arrived at the counter, the receiver asked who accompanied him.

"I'm by myself." He showed her his identification.

She examined his document and input into her databoard. "You are the son of Dr. Trodner Gravton. You will need to wait for him. As a juvenile, you cannot leave unaccompanied," she explained.

"But he can't leave now, he's a doctor," he pleaded.

"I'm sorry, I don't have you on this manifest so you will need to wait for him. Next." She looked at the individual behind him in line.

Keyloi stepped aside and walked through the crowded lobby to exit the building. *I don't want to ever see him or be near him again. How can I evacuate?* He walked back to the colony pondering what he could do.

They wouldn't leave me if I was by myself in the last shuttle. He will already be gone, and I could be a last survivor. When I get there, I'll talk to someone about him. He determined he would expose the doctor. All he must do is wait. *That's easy enough.*

As he walked toward the Commons, an explosion and groundquake happened thirty meters in front of him. A huge monolith rose in the Commons. He stood there in disbelief. *What is that, and how did that happen?* He crept closer to the epicenter and saw colonists scrambling everywhere trying to get away from it. The monolith destroyed the left section of the administrative building. It stood thirty to forty meters tall, was round, and looked like stone or rock or compacted dirt. The odor was sickening. *That's where that smell is coming from.*

Chaos was everywhere. Colonists were running in all directions. Very quickly, the Scouts and military arrived. They talked to everyone and directed them toward the evacuation point. Keyloi tried to understand what was going on, but all he gleaned from the information was that they were in danger, and an evacuation was eminent.

He heard that a monster was coming. *I would rather be killed by a monster than live with one.* He walked away from the turmoil to the edge of the Commons. He watched humanoids coming and going here and there. Some were confused and stared at the menacing tower. He saw the emergency workers showing others which way to go. He stood still, watching the scene.

A verbal announcement was made to go inside the units and leave all lights illuminated for the entire night. No one was allowed outside after dark. *Were they stopping the evacuations during the night?*

After a few minutes, he decided to go to the cleaning closet. He could hide out there until everything calmed down. Keyloi felt that was his safe place. Nothing could harm him while he was inside his lair. It was getting dusk. He entered, locked both doors, and turned on the lights.

He made his bed and lay down. He got up and turned off the lights. *There are no windows in this room so nothing can get in. Who will know I'm even here?*

His mind drifted on what he should do. After some thought, he devised a plan to wait at the colony until very few humanoids are left on planet. He would then make his way to the air portal to get on the last shuttle. He rested.

Section 18

Keyloi woke and felt miserable, but he thought he would look outside to see if it was daytime. As he opened the door, Capria's light flooded the room. He immediately smelled the same odor he noticed just the morning prior. He stuck his head out the door. Capria's light was around noon.

A few humanoids scampered here and there. Some with their belongings walked toward the air portal. He stretched, bent over, and twisted. He felt very tired and unrested. He exited the closet and looked around. He heard an amplified speaker state that all humanoids need to be ready for departure and should proceed toward the air shuttle soon.

He thought this was a good time to go since the doctor most likely had already left. He started toward the air portal but saw Dr. Kelba a little distance from him. He ran in the opposite direction and jumped behind a unit to avoid the doctor from seeing him. He snuck to the other side of the structure and peeked around the corner to seek the doctor's location. He saw him walking toward the undisturbed side of the administrative building. *Is he not leaving yet?* Keyloi's hopes dropped. He wished the doctor would evacuate, and as his shuttle was leaving, Keyloi would be ready to take the next flight. He leaned his back against the unit and rested his head on the structure.

***

He opened his eyes. He had fallen asleep. He rubbed his eyes and face and yawned. *Why am I so tired?* Keyloi needed to keep an eye on the doctor to see when he would leave. He searched for a good place to keep watch without being seen. He found a unit that was already abandoned and entered it. He went to one of the windows where he would have a good view of the medical center and a window on another side to view the admin building. He sat and watched the admin building for his abuser's appearance.

It seemed like hours passed as he watched. He saw a few humanoids on their way to the air portal. As time passed, even less traffic was seen. He had not seen the doctor. He nodded a couple of times and had to move around to stay awake. He moved to view the medical center, but it had very little foot traffic. *Where is he?* He squatted down against the wall to watch the medical facility.

***

Keyloi slowly opened his eyes. It was dark. His eyes sprang open, and he quickly stood up. "Oh, no!" He moved closer to the window. He ran out the front door into the darkness. He looked into the sky to notice a shuttle exiting the atmosphere.

No lights were shining from any structures or street posts. *Where is everyone?* "Hello? Can anyone hear me?" he yelled as he walked toward the medical facility.

Silence. Then he heard a faint yipping noise in front of him. He faced the sound and saw a movement above the surrounding units. It was nearing him. He quickly ran back into the unit. He slammed the door just before a loud crash hit it. The door pushed him across the room. He hurried into one of the rooms and closed the interior door. He heard something banging against the window. The window stayed firm against the assault. Something was outside trying to get him. He ran back into the main room at the same time as the door crashed open. He screamed. A creature with a long neck and wings was trying to get through the doorway. It shrieked as it struggled while stretching its neck toward Keyloi.

Keyloi ran to the relieving room, closed the door, and locked it. He searched around with his hands and discovered a cabinet was near the door. He pushed it over in front of the door. Then, he got in front of it and pushed with all he could toward the door.

A loud commotion accompanied by squeals was heard outside the door. He sat down on the floor with his back to the cabinet and his feet stretched out toward the relieving station for leverage. Keyloi pushed with all his might. The door bounced and shook as the creature pummeled it. He wanted to scream but knew it would not help the situation. The creature's squeals and pounding on the door were unnerving. He held tight.

Soon, his legs began to tire, and his muscles began to

ache. *Will this ever let up?*

After what seemed like a lifetime, the pounding stopped. He still maintained his stance. It grew quiet. Keyloi didn't move. *Maybe it thinks I'm gone.* He listened carefully, and all he heard was faint yips. He remained on alert.

He waited for a long time before he relaxed his legs. There was no sense of time inside the windowless room without a timepiece. He relaxed without moving from the cabinet. He must keep those monsters out of the room at all costs.

Hours passed, and the sounds and squeals had ceased. He thought he would be brave and open the door. He stretched. His legs needed the activity. He knew he couldn't stay in that room another night. He moved the cabinet and slowly opened the door to an empty room. Welcoming rays of light invaded the small room from the destroyed front door and two windows that were on the adjacent walls. He went to view the outside scene. *How did I get out of that?* He shook his head.

He decided to search the clinic. Maybe something was left that he could use as a weapon. After arriving, he quietly walked down the hallway toward Dr. Kelba's office. He surveyed the scene. Nothing out of the ordinary, so he slowly opened the door.

He went to the instrument cabinet to search, but a chair was blocking the door. He scooted it to one side and began his search in the cabinet. There was nothing of any use as a weapon. He stood up and looked around. A closet door handle made a noise, and the door slowly opened a small bit. Keyloi froze.

What's going on? Is something in there? He listened intently. *I hope there isn't a monster in there. Monsters don't open doors.*

He cautiously approached the door, and it began to open wider.

It's coming out! Fear struck the youth. He put his hand on the door to stop it from opening. There was pressure as he held the door. The door began closing.

What? Why is it closing? Keyloi grabbed the edge of the door to see what was causing it to move. An explosion occurred. He jumped back into the corner. He looked around, but there was nowhere he could hide. He would have to pass the door to get out of the room.

Maybe there is someone in there.

Instinctively, he asked, "Hello?"

He heard a slight groan then a humanoid voice asked, "Who's there?"

"I'm Keyloi Gravton." He loved using his first name but automatically said his faux last name since that was all he knew.

The voice replied, "Braven Triton. I'm a Scout."

A Scout? Like a Discovery Scout? Keyloi stuck his head around the corner of the doorway to see a young man on the floor.

"Really?" he asked in surprise.

They stared at each other for a moment. The adult wore a

dirty Scout uniform. He had dark hair with a light brown complexion. He was holding his side. *He must be hurt.*

"I didn't know you were in there. I've been hiding all night to stay away from the monsters." Keyloi was excited to find another humanoid.

The man groaned and then asked, "Where are the others?"

"They've all gone. I saw one of the last shuttles flying away yesterday afternoon and didn't know where to go. I'm glad I found you. How soon can we leave?"

Keyloi helped the adult get up. He grunted and bent over toward his left side.

"Are you okay?"

"I'll be fine," the Scout responded.

You don't look like you'll be fine. You need some pain meds.

"You saw the last shuttle? How do you know it was the last?"

Keyloi hesitated and then answered, "I went to the air portal. No one was there, and all the shuttles were gone." Keyloi lied to hide that he was hiding from his father. W*hy is this Scout still here? I thought everyone was gone. I wonder if he was cut off from his unit or was left to fight those monsters by himself so everyone could leave. If anyone was here with me, I'm glad it's a Scout.*

"Why are you still here?" he asked.

"Long story," Braven grunted. "I'll explain later."

"What are we going to do?"

"Well, first, I'm hurting and need something for this pain. And I haven't eaten in a while. I'm going to see if I can find something here and then go to the Lounge."

"I can help with the pain." Keyloi took off down the hallway to the supply cabinet where he found some dologra. It was only a few rooms away, so he found the cabinet, made sure he had a dologra dose, and closed the cabinet. He ran back to his newly found hero.

"Here's a dose of dologra. It's a pain eliminator."

Braven examined the meds. "Where did you get this, and how do you know what to get?"

"My dad is a physician." *Well, he's not my real dad, but you don't need to know that.* "This was his room. I've been his assistant this past year. Do you want me to administer it?" Keyloi was excited that he could work like a real doctor.

Braven looked at him and slowly nodded.

Keyloi administered the dose like he saw it happen so many times. "That will last for twelve to fifteen hours."

"Well, aren't you handy to have around?"

"You just say it because it's true." A grin came over the boy's face. "I heard some of the others at school say that. I think it's funny."

He looked at the area of Braven's pain. *His ribs are broken.* "Probably broken ribs. Do you have problems breathing?"

Braven nodded.

"Normally, they could just repair your bones, but they took the Cylinder. You will need regular doses until your ribs are healed. I know where the medicine is kept when you need some more. For some reason, they must have left it here."

"That already feels much better," the adult said. "Let's go find something to eat."

Inside the Lounge, everything was gone. They searched in the cabinets and storage rooms. Nothing.

After their hunt, Keyloi said, "They took everything. I know where we can find something."

They returned to the medical facility and went down to the end of the hallway to a breakroom. He looked inside one of the lower cabinets where there were still a few food packets left.

"I noticed these this morning when I was searching for the meds. They must have just missed it or run out of time and didn't clean it all out. The same for the dologra. There was an entire cabinet of medicines left."

"Good break for us." Braven dove into one of the packaged meals. "By the way, why are you still here?"

Keyloi quickly thought of some story to elaborate. He didn't know this adult and didn't trust him. He explained that he was scheduled for the next to last shuttle but wanted to stay around for his dad that was leaving on the last. He hid out but fell asleep. When he awoke, the last shuttle had taken off. He hesitated. "I'm glad I found you. I don't know what to do."

"Your father left without you?" the Scout asked.

"Uh," Keyloi thought, "I was supposed to go on the shuttle before his." *Keyloi lied again. He didn't like to fabricate stories but felt he needed to.*

"We'll stay together and figure this out. You sure you haven't seen anyone else?" Braven asked.

He was thrilled that this Scout wanted to stay with him. Keyloi had a warm welcome from him but was afraid to trust him. "Not yet, but I haven't moved around the colony much."

After eating, Keyloi followed the Scout to the Scout camp. He had never been there before and was excited to go. The ground was pushed up inside their camp. Braven surveyed the scene and decided not to enter the compound.

"Hey, do you have a databoard?" he asked Keyloi.

He wished he had one but answered, "I'm only twelve."

"Do you know of any electronics anywhere?"

Keyloi thought about it. He hadn't seen any in the medical facility or anywhere else he had been. "No," he responded.

Braven said he had lost his databoard, and they needed to get word to the space portal. Keyloi didn't know what to say. If they couldn't let anyone know, they may be there for the rest of their lives.

Braven suggested they look around the colony to see if they could find anything to send a message. They walked over to the air portal, but a monolith stood right where the last air shuttle left. There was another one close to the main building.

Braven didn't want to venture too close to those monoliths, so they turned back toward the Commons. They searched through all the buildings that still stood, but there was nothing to be found. They went to the nearby lodging units, but they were clean. They searched throughout the day.

Keyloi happened upon a small power light. "Look what I found." He turned it on and held up the device.

"Great find. Those monsters don't like the light, so it will help."

Keyloi felt like he had accomplished something good, and that Braven was proud of him. He liked impressing the Scout but was still cautious of their friendship.

They returned to the medical center and searched for rooms with no windows. Braven suggested two doors so they could escape if the caprodomes got through one. Keyloi thought that was a great idea.

Even though they searched every room, they turned up without finding their intended location. They settled on a relieving room with no windows and one door. They would have to make sure they keep the door blocked. The room was large enough for them to stretch out for sleep. Keyloi didn't suggest his hiding place in case he needed to get away from this adult.

"We found a safe place, now we need something to sleep on and some food," the Scout said.

They looked in several rooms and found a couple of blankets and medical scrub jackets.

"These will do, now for some food." Braven said.

Keyloi led the way to the snack room where they found what they needed. They returned to their lair about time Capria was about to set.

They settled in while they still had light before closing the door. They sat silently until the Scout started asking questions.

"Where is your planet?"

"I was born on Radzier. Couldn't you tell by my handsome complexion?" The boy giggled.

Braven smiled big. "I have a question. How do you say the name of your planet and your star? I can never tell the difference."

"Non-Radzierians usually can't. The star is pronounced Radzier, but the planet is Radzier."

Braven gave a crooked smile. "That sounds the same to me."

The boy articulated the names. The slight intonation of his pronunciation could have been easily missed if he hadn't pointed it out.

"I hear the difference now. I've always relied on context clues." He chuckled.

After a little while of small talk, Braven asked the youth if he wanted first or second shift.

"Uh, I don't care. What do I have to do?"

"Just stay awake and wake me up if you hear anything," Braven instructed.

"I'm not sleepy now, so right now," Keyloi said.

Braven told him that when he started getting too sleepy to wake him. He would take the rest of the night. The youth agreed.

Keyloi sat quietly. The Scout grew still, and only quiet breathing was heard.

He thought of where they could find a databoard, weapons, or a good place at night. Those monsters would wake up at any minute, and he didn't want to hear them like he had last night. He wondered what they ate when there were no humanoids available.

Keyloi thought of how fortunate he was to find a Scout. And not just any Scout but one like Braven. He was so smart and knew what to do. He would protect him from the monsters. A sense of peace but caution settled on him. Braven was an adult and Keyloi didn't know him very well. He seemed like a good man, but so had his adoptive father. He wanted the feeling of peace to continue.

Hopefully, we can get off the planet tomorrow. When we get to the space portal… Keyloi stopped. He knew when they arrived at the space portal, he would have to go back with Dr. Kelba. *I won't go back with him. I can't be around the doctor anymore.*

Tears welled up in his eyes. He wiped them off. They just

kept coming. He lay down and let the tears flow. He missed peace. He missed love. He was lonely. His mind drifted until he rested.

***

Keyloi felt something tap his foot. He jumped up against the wall and looked around. He rubbed his eyes. "What time is it?"

"It's morning. Let's start searching the units to the east," came the quick response. Braven groaned.

Keyloi noticed that the Scout was having pain again. "You need another dose of dologra. It's probably past time by now."

"Let me look around first." Braven reached for the door handle. He slowly unlatched the door and carefully eased it open. A sliver of light broke the deep darkness of the room. They felt relieved.

Braven swung the door open wide to reveal a caprodome staring at him.

Section 19

Braven slammed the door. Keyloi screamed. He retreated to the rear wall. Unexpected fear shot though his being.

"It's daytime!" Keyloi strongly whispered. "Why is that thing still outside?"

"Get out your power light."

Keyloi fumbled in his pockets and dropped the light on the floor. He searched around to retrieve it. He hunkered against the back wall with the light shining on the Scout at the door.

Braven held tightly to the handle. He reached for his stun pistol and readied it.

Keyloi was terrified. He started sweating and breathing extremely hard. He made a whimper before he realized it.

Braven mouthed the words, "It's okay." Then he whispered, "Breathe."

There was a harsh scraping sound outside the door and then silence. They waited. Braven put his ear to the door. He heard nothing. They waited a little longer. Everything was silent, and they had calmed down.

Braven quietly said, "I'm going to check if it's still out

there."

Fear captured Keyloi. "No," he shook his head. "Don't open it," he pleaded.

The Scout waited a few more minutes. He then said the monster must be gone because he didn't hear anything. He readied his stun pistol and prepared for a confrontation. Keyloi froze with his power light directed at the door.

Braven slowly opened the door. He searched as much of the room as he could in all directions as the door opened. He listened for any evidence of the creature. There was nothing.

The Scout slowly opened the door until they could exit. He motioned for Keyloi, but the boy was not interested in leaving their saferoom. Hesitantly, Keyloi slowly exited the room and hurried to Braven's side.

Braven put the palm side of his fingers over his mouth as a quiet sign and pointed to the door. He made his way to the exit into the hallway; Keyloi shadowed him.

Braven opened the door and looked out. He took Keyloi's power light and shined into the hallway. He then backed up and closed the door.

"There may be a dozen caprodomes in the hallway," he whispered quietly.

Keyloi's heart stopped. He stared at the door and then at the Scout. *How could he be so brave when we are about to be eaten?*

Braven touched his arm. He mouthed, "Breathe."

Keyloi didn't realize he had stopped. He exhaled and whispered, "Why are they here?"

After a short pause, the Scout responded, "They need a dark place to rest during the day. The dark hallway with no windows is a perfect place for them."

They opened one of the waist-high windows in the room and looked around. Keyloi leaped out onto the ground. A simple hustaka move. He noticed that Braven was having a difficult time getting out due to his injury. Keyloi climbed back inside the window and knelt on his hands and knees in front of the window.

"Step on my lower back, on my hips, to raise yourself," he instructed.

"I'm too heavy for you," Braven protested.

"Do it. We need to get out of here."

Keyloi could feel Braven's foot bracing on his lower back and hips and when he pulled himself up enough to exit the window. He jumped outside the window and let out a groan. Keyloi jumped back out the window.

Keyloi looked at Braven and knew he was in pain.

"You need another dose." He returned inside the window, quickly retrieved a dose of dologra and two food packets. As soon as he got out the window, he administered the dose.

After a few minutes, Braven said, "Amazing how quickly that works." He inhaled deeply but then coughed and grabbed his side.

"Don't overdo it."

Braven winced and agreed.

They decided to walk toward the air portal. Keyloi was trying to chat, but Braven didn't seem to hear him as he surveyed the area. They saw the destruction the monoliths caused. They knew the caprodomes were out during the night, so they were safe during the day. As for food, if they were not successful in finding any, they would only have flora which wasn't very nutritious. They arrived outside the air portal Perimeter. The monolith made a big mess on the shuttle pad.

Keyloi sighed, "Could it get any worse?"

A small groundquake happened.

That was bizarre. Keyloi widened his eyes and looked around. "I won't ask that anymore."

Braven chuckled.

Keyloi couldn't understand how he could be so calm and easy-going.

"It doesn't look like an air shuttle will be coming, and without communications, we don't know when anyone will come to rescue us," Braven stated.

"So, what about the caprodomes?"

"They'll come back at night, so we will make sure we are somewhere safe before Capria sets."

Keyloi's mind bounced. "You mean we won't be leaving today?"

"Not right now. Maybe the military will send a scouting drone to check things out," Braven thought aloud.

Hopelessness drenched Keyloi. He looked toward the ground.

"It's okay, Keyloi," the Scout encouraged. "We'll figure out something. Just stay near me, and if you see anything out of the norm, let me know."

Keyloi chuckled. "Um, there are a lot of things out of the norm."

Braven laughed aloud. "You are so right." The two shared a time of laughter.

Braven said they needed to return to the colony and find food and medicine.

Keyloi threw his hands up in front of him. "I'm not going back in that building."

"Okay, so tell me where you found the meds and food, and I'll go get it."

"You won't make it without me."

"Why not?" Braven looked over at him.

Keyloi sighed, "I'll have to show you."

"Let's go then."

Keyloi hesitated. He was afraid of going back inside the medical building where the caprodomes were sleeping. He sighed. He was reluctant then sighed again. "Let's go. While we are there, we need to get all the doses and clear out the food locker. I don't want to go back in there with those monsters."

"Good thinking." Braven said.

The two returned to the medical building and looked

through a window. Keyloi moved to the next window and the next until he found the intended room.

"There it is." He pointed to some closet doors and a set of cabinets.

Braven tried the window, but it was immovable.

"Can you just break it?"

"Windows don't break"—Braven raised his eyes and grinned—"unless the building is toppled by a monolith." He smirked.

Keyloi didn't think his response was funny.

Braven took his stun pistol and slammed it at the bottom corner of the window. Nothing. He hit it again. Nothing.

"You're right, windows don't break. So, how can we get in?" Keyloi asked.

"I don't know."

Braven slowly walked to the end of the building. He looked inside and frowned. "We cannot get to the meds or that food right now. So, let's continue our search elsewhere for food and communications equipment."

They headed toward the western region. After visiting two dozen empty units with no success, they returned to the Commons. They discussed a safe shelter for the night. Both had thoughts, but neither was sure their place was safe enough.

They wandered around the structures and looked for a room without windows but with an exterior door so the creatures wouldn't block it while they slept. *That sounds a lot like the closet I used to hide from Dr. Kelba.* After a pointed search, Keyloi led him to an entrance to the educational building that opened into a mechanical room. A door opened into the hallway. There were no windows and plenty of room for them both to stretch out for rest.

"Perfect!" Braven exclaimed. "Now we need to fortify it." He then let out a soft groan and grimaced. "I've got to sit for a few minutes." He sat down to hold his side. "Why am I hurting so soon?"

Keyloi remembered that there was another way into the medical room with the pain meds. He knew he could jump in and get out without awaking any of the monsters.

"Hey, rest a minute. I'll be back." At that, he took off running back to the medical facility.

"Wait. Where are you going?" Braven called.

He heard the Scout but thought he would fill him in when he got back. He needed to get the meds soon. He saw how much pain the Scout was in, and he needed help.

On the way to the center, he realized that he must have given Braven a smaller dose of dologra. He saw the medicine's name but didn't pay attention to the amount in the syringe.

As he drew near the medical facility, he could feel the warm sunshine. He wished there was more wind and shade. There's nowhere to go to get out of Capria's exposure except inside a building. He recalled all the large trees in the Radzierian forest.

As he got closer, he circled to the rear. He remembered a window that the medical staff used to open to talk with others that were outside the back of the building. Sometimes it would be open all day long. *Maybe they forgot to close it.*

He saw the window and checked to see if it was open.

"Max!" he said under his breath. He was impressed but didn't want to make any noise that would wake the monsters.

He pulled himself up to the window. Clear. He lifted his leg around and swung it inside. Quietly, he got his feet on the floor and stealthily moved to the breezeway. Still clear. He entered the door immediately on his right, and there was his treasure cabinet.

He quickly emptied the essential meds and food packages into a large towel he found by the unit. Folding the top together to create a tote, he returned to the window, jumped to the ground, and off he went to rejoin his new Scout friend. He didn't want him to be hurting so badly.

As he closed in on his destination, he noticed something moving at the Scout's feet. Braven was watching it closely. *What could that be?*

Keyloi looked intently at a small creature. It looked like a fauna that he saw at the edge of the forest at Dr. Kelba's home. *Is that a limya? What's a limya doing here?*

The small creature had light brown fur all over its body but no fur on its head. It had four legs and a tail. Its neck was slightly longer than the limya he had seen.

"Is that a limya? Where did it come from?" Keyloi lay his baggage on the ground. He was amazed to see a small limya-looking creature since there were no other creatures anywhere on the planet. He bent down as it playfully came up to him.

"It's friendly." Keyloi was excited.

"I'm not sure you should be playing with it. We don't know what it is or its origin."

"It looks like a limya from my planet. They are playful, and some humanoids keep them for comfort and play. This doesn't look exactly like a limya, but that's what it is."

Braven displayed concern as he looked around. "How did it get here? And why is it just now showing up?"

"Oh, I got some more meds for you," Keyloi forgot all about Braven's pain.

"Why am I hurting so soon? The last doses helped all day."

"This morning's dose must have been smaller. This one is for twelve hours."

Keyloi opened and administered the painkiller to the Scout. Within minutes, Braven felt the relief start.

"And I got something to eat," Keyloi said as he returned to play with the friendly creature.

Braven asked, "Where did you get it?"

"Uh, I found a way back into the medical room," he replied without looking up. He had fun playing with the limya. It seemed to show him love in its own way.

"Keyloi," Braven chided, "you can't just run off like that without at least letting me know where you're going. You can't get around those caprodomes. We must be a team if we're going to survive."

A feeling of disappointment came over the youth. "I'm sorry, Tani." He continued playing with the fauna without looking up.

"We need to prepare our shelter for the night. Capria will be disappearing soon."

Keyloi followed Braven but was upset with him. *I risked my life to get meds for him, and he jumps at me.* He kept his mind on his playful newfound friend.

They returned to their lair and stored the items inside. The little limya followed in its playful manner but stayed outside the room. Braven checked his stun pistol and Keyloi's power light.

Keyloi sat with the limya bouncing all around him. It licked his hands and face. It let Keyloi hold him close. It lay on Keyloi's leg as the lad straightened its fur with his fingers. He loved the companionship of his new little friend.

Capria began to settle. Braven said it was time they needed to get inside. As the two entered the doorway, the limya stayed outside the door. Keyloi coaxed it in, but it refused to enter and only squeaked.

"Why won't it come in?" he asked.

Suddenly, the small creature took off running. Keyloi felt lost.

"Limya! Limya! Where is he going? You can't go anywhere?" Keyloi started back outside when the Scout grabbed his arm. "We can't leave it outside tonight," Keyloi begged.

"That thing has a safe place because the caprodomes haven't found it yet. Let it go for tonight, and we'll see what happens in the morning."

"No, it needs our help." Keyloi was upset. *Why don't you understand?*

"No, it does not." Braven's voice was harsh. "We tried, but it took off. I would rather the monsters eat that thing than you or me."

"No, it won't survive." Keyloi's heart ached.

"It has survived this far. It knows what it's doing. It has been safe for its whole life. We will probably see it in the morning."

Keyloi stopped. Braven locked both doors and would not allow him to go get it.

Keyloi just stood and stared at the Scout. *It's going to get eaten. We can't leave it outside no matter what he says. I can't believe he will let it die. It loves me, and I don't want it to die.* Tears came to his eyes.

Section 20

Keyloi lay with his back to the Scout. He was angry that Braven
wouldn't let that tiny creature come into their protection. In his
mind, he could hear its yips, cries for help. Tears continued. *How
can he let the limya get killed? It needed help, and he doesn't
even care.*

"Keyloi," Braven quietly called.

The youth did not verbally response. *I'm not talking to
you. You think you're right and that I don't know what I'm
talking about. The only little creature on this entire planet, and
you are going to let it get killed by those monsters.*

"Well, get some rest while you can," Braven whispered.

*How can I get some rest when the limya is being
terrorized by those monsters before they tear him apart for a
meal?* A quick wave a heat washed over his face. His breathing
was elevated.

*You're just like all adults, do it your way no matter who it
hurts. Why couldn't I have kept it as my companion? What would
it have hurt? It's not fair. You have your family, but I only have
... nobody. Dr. Kelba's not my father. I'm sure my real father*

loved me. He wouldn't have treated me like this. Hopelessness exploded. A river of water ran down his cheeks.

Keyloi refused to wipe away the moisture. He didn't want to move. He didn't even want to talk.

After a little while, he heard a faint sound outside. *Those monsters are here.* He didn't move. It happened again but louder. It sounded like the limya. He waited and listened intently. The anticipation was strong. There it was again. It was the limya.

Keyloi raised up and wiped his eyes. "Is that the limya?"

"Quiet," Braven whispered.

The noise grew until it sounded outside their door.

"It *is* the limya." Keyloi jumped up and moved to the door. *It came back for us to help it.* He turned on his power light and illuminated the door.

Braven grabbed the boy's arm. "You are not opening that door," he demanded.

Anger arose in Keyloi. He stared at the Scout. "But the limya is outside. It needs us to protect it."

The squeaking continued.

"You can't let the limya get killed." He reached for the door handle.

Braven grabbed his arm. "We are not opening that door. Capria is gone, and the caprodomes are ready to go out."

"I don't hear any caprodomes, but I hear the limya pleading for help."

Braven stopped. He looked at the door and then back to

154

Keyloi. He drew his ear closer to the door. The tiny squeak continued.

After a long moment of silence, Braven said, "I'll check to see if it's okay. Any sign of danger, this door closes and will not be opened. Agreed?" He pointed his finger at Keyloi.

"Of course," Keyloi responded. His senses intensified with the thought of having the limya in his arms.

Braven took his stun pistol in one hand and held the doorknob with the other. Keyloi's breathing increased; his heart pounded. The squeaking beckoned him. He held his power light steady.

Braven slowly unlatched the door and opened it a few centimeters. They saw nothing. They heard the squeaks behind the door. Keyloi moved toward the door with anticipation. *Open it wider. It's right there,* Keyloi directed Braven in his mind. He leaned closer toward the door.

Braven carefully opened the door enough to reveal the limya. Keyloi's heart jumped with joy. His breathing increased. *Get it. Get it.* Braven laid down the stun pistol and held out his hand to get it.

Suddenly, a rushing snap hit Braven's hand. A caprodome screamed and shot at the door, but Braven slammed it. The monster started pounding on the door.

Keyloi screamed and jumped against the wall.

"Quiet!" Braven strongly whispered.

The pounding grew louder. More of the creatures showed

up. Braven held the door handle tightly.

Keyloi was terrified. He hunkered down at the back wall as far away from that door as possible. The interior door near him was locked. Braven held tightly as the creatures pounded on the exterior door even though the door was locked.

The hammering continued seemingly for hours. Braven continued holding the handle and could see it was still locked. He kept his grip solid.

"What happened to the limya?" Keyloi asked.

"The limya must have been a decoy. It was working with the caprodomes."

"What? I don't understand."

"The limya survives the daylight to scout for suspected victims and then brings the caprodomes at night," Braven explained.

"I didn't know. I almost got us killed." Keyloi felt guilt invade him.

"We are alive, and I mean to keep it that way."

Pounding began on the interior door. Keyloi jumped toward Braven.

"Hold that handle, and do not let it unlock," Braven ordered.

Keyloi hesitated. He didn't want to get anywhere close to them.

"Get that handle now. We need to hold them off." Braven raised his whispered voice.

Keyloi jumped back to the door and grabbed the handle as directed. He felt the poundings jar his shoulder.

"They know we're in here and are adamant about getting to us. We need to hold them off until Capria rises," the Scout directed.

"How long will that be?"

"Who knows? We'll have to wait until these creatures are tired or Capria rises and then all the pounding will stop."

Hours passed. Keyloi held his door handle but was getting tired. He wanted to stop but held on.

The pounding slowed. It sounded as though only one creature pounded each door rather than the multitude. The yips were less frequent. Soon, the hammering ceased.

It was quiet.

Braven said they could release the handles. Capria must be rising to scare the monsters off. They sat back and relaxed. Keyloi shook and stretched his hands. His arms hurt and even his back was feeling tight. Braven was rubbing his shoulders. Keyloi just wanted to get some rest.

Keyloi thought about his tiny potential friend. "I can't believe the limya was part of it." *Did it want me to be eaten?*

"I can't believe the creatures were able to strategize that way," Braven added.

Keyloi thought of the limya. What did it eat? "What do the caprodomes eat if they only eat humanoids or fauna? There are none on this planet. Well, except you and me." Keyloi wondered aloud.

Braven chuckled. "That's a question that no one knows the answer. They may be omnivores and use flora as nourishment as well. I haven't heard of anyone being able to successfully study them. Why don't we just rest rather than leave the room. We need to get some sleep."

Keyloi thought that was a great idea. He found a comfortable spot, and soon, he was fast asleep.

Section 21

Keyloi awakened. He stretched and rubbed his eyes and face. His shoulders were sore, and hands were tight. He opened and closed his fists and stretched again.

"Oh, I am so sore." Keyloi rubbed his shoulders and neck.

"Yes, it was because we held the doors so tightly last night for so long. We probably need a different place to stay tonight. They know where we are and will be back."

Keyloi could see that the Scout was in pain, so he delivered another painkiller.

"There are only two more doses. These last twelve hours each, so after tomorrow you won't have any relief."

"They've been good for me. I'll try to make them last longer."

"Not with you crawling through windows and fighting off caprodomes." He was impressed by how Braven took charge and protected them from the monsters when he himself was so afraid.

"You have a good point." Braven chuckled.

They gathered their goods to leave. Braven said they should try to enter the air portal to see if there was any way to communicate. They would need to stay clear of the monolith and work around the debris.

As they approached the portal, they entered the Perimeter and scouted the area. There was a monolith outside the air portal, but the structure was basically intact with no visible physical damage.

After surveying the scene, Braven said, "Let's go see what we can find inside."

They pried open the doors. After they entered, Braven secured the doors. They saw what looked like a quick evacuation had occurred. Furniture was disheveled. Personal belongings still sat beside benches. They searched through the abandoned personal effects but found no databoard.

They continued their search, opening doors throughout the structure—offices, storeroom, janitorial closet, breakroom, equipment room, relief station, conference room. Finally, a communications room.

They put their treasures on a table in the communications room and sorted through each item. Nothing. Braven started trying to get any equipment in the communications room to work but had no luck.

"Power source. We need a power source," Braven thought aloud. They searched the wall and floor panels to find a power source. Nothing. "I know they have backup power somewhere." They scanned the room.

They rummaged through drawers and cabinets, opened

equipment doors, and looked along walls, ceilings, and floors. Nothing.

"Why does this have to be so difficult?" Braven mumbled to himself.

"Do you think they took all the power blocks with them?" Keyloi tried to help.

"Probably. They were the last to leave and had plenty of time to pack. If we could just find a simple databoard."

They exited the next door, which opened the conference room. They did a thorough search but found nothing. Room after room, they hunted for something useful.

They entered the breakroom and found some nourishment packets that were left. They sat at one of the tables and quietly enjoyed their meals.

"What if we don't find anything? Will we be here forever?" Keyloi questioned.

After a short pause, Braven answered. "I'm not sure. I've never encountered an evacuation before. I don't know if anyone returns to make sure everyone was evacuated or not."

"Don't they know we're missing and will come look for us?"

"Well, in my case, they probably thought I was killed when the monolith erupted. That's when I lost my databoard. When I awoke, I was covered with debris on top of a building. I was alone. In your case, I'm not sure."

Keyloi lowered his head. He hadn't told Braven the truth.

He hadn't told anyone the truth since he had been on planet. He was tired of the lies.

"I didn't tell you the truth," he quietly admitted.

Braven turned and looked at him. "About what? Is your dad not a physician?"

"Oh, no, he is. He's not my real father. I didn't want to stay with him. When I realized everyone was leaving, it was too late."

"What do you mean you didn't want to stay with him?"

Keyloi was afraid of getting in trouble. *Dr. Kelba said the authorities were looking for me, too.* "Oh, I was just mad at him. It's nothing."

Braven asked a couple more questions that Keyloi didn't want to talk about. They continued eating their meals in silence.

After a few minutes, Braven quickly got up and made his way over to a shelf. He raised a towel and found a databoard. He tried to power it up, but it had no power.

"It needs recharging. I'll put it in Capria's light for a little while." He hurried to a door which opened onto an eastern veranda. Keyloi was excited and followed. He placed the databoard so it could receive the most afternoon light. They waited. It began charging.

The two cheered.

"Now we need to wait for a charge, send a message, and then hope for someone to come get us."

As they stood outside, they heard a small squeak.

They both dropped to the ground.

"Get inside, quickly."

They reentered the building and heard the noise again as the door closed.

"It knows we're here," Keyloi whispered.

"Yes, it does. We need to keep it from exposing our location. Let's go get it and lock it in one of the rooms," Braven said.

"Good idea."

They opened the door to find the little limya dancing around. It was so playful and enticing. Keyloi exited and played with it for a few seconds. He picked it up and held it at arm's length. He didn't want to get bitten or attacked. "Now, where do we put it?" he asked.

"We need to find a room where we will not be. They can probably hear his squeaks, so it needs to be a quiet room."

"What about the communications room? Aren't they usually soundproofed?"

"You're just a sharp fellow today. Let's do it," Braven commented.

Keyloi felt a spark of pride.

They carried the little critter to the room and went inside. There were no windows, and it had insulated walls. It was a perfect place to stash their tattletale.

They put down the limya and closed the door. The squeaking disappeared. They listened intently but could hear nothing.

"Perfect! Good job, Keyloi. Now we need to find a shelter of our own."

Keyloi enjoyed the Scout complimenting him. He felt like Braven listened to him and allowed him to help.

They looked in the other rooms. Most had windows, only the equipment and the janitor's rooms did not.

"I'm tired of sleeping in closets," Keyloi said.

Braven chuckled. "We'll stay in the equipment room."

It was getting dusk. Braven got the databoard and went inside. He closed and locked all exterior doors. They entered the equipment room and settled in for the night.

Braven took the databoard and powered it up.

"What?" he muttered. A minutes later, he exclaimed, "What's going on?"

"What's wrong?" Keyloi inquired.

"Oh, just not working as fast as I want it to," the Scout mumbled.

After a minute, Braven asked, "Keyloi, what is your dad's contact name?"

He didn't want Braven to contact Dr. Kelba. He never wanted to see him again. "I don't know," he answered.

Braven looked at him. "What's his name? I can find him that way."

"That's okay. I'm sure I'll see him when we get there," Keyloi mumbled. He was concerned. How could he get away from that man and not get in trouble himself?

Braven paused. "Keyloi?"

"I don't want to talk about it." Keyloi looked down at his knee. The feeling of hopelessness overwhelmed him. He wanted to be free, but if he told anyone about what Dr. Kelba and Keyloi had done, everyone in the multiverse would know and hate him.

Braven responded, "Well, I should be getting something from HQ or my parents soon. I already told them about you."

Oh, no. They will know I'm still alive and will tell him. What will he tell the officials about me? How can I get out of this? I hate that man and am tired of living with him. He could feel tears welling.

"Braven, it's okay," he finally said. "He's just not very nice to me."

"What do you mean? Does he abuse you?" Braven sounded sincere.

Keyloi lowered his head. *I shouldn't have said that.* Feelings of distraught swept over him.

"Hey Keyloi, what's going on?"

I can't tell him. What will he think of me? "Nothing. It's okay," his voice cracked.

"Keyloi, if you need to talk about something, I am your only listener."

"Maybe later." He looked up.

"When you're ready to talk, I'm right here for you. I'll see what I can do to help."

What do I say? I don't want Braven to hate me. I'm so ashamed.

The two sat quietly without speaking. The quietness in the room was intense. Keyloi's mind swirled with hurt and guilt, longing to be free from his internal pain. He couldn't stop the wetness from flooding his eyes.

"Hey, why don't you go ahead and get some rest," the Scout suggested. "Hopefully, we won't have any problems tonight."

Keyloi lay down and turned away from Braven. He tried to stop thinking about his past experiences on the planet. The feelings of wanting to tell someone versus the shame he could experience tormented his thoughts. Would his life always be like this? Would he ever be free to have fun like he used to have?

He could hear Braven tapping on the databoard. *He must be telling someone about him to notify Dr. Kelba that he was here. I will have to go back to live with him. I do not want that to happen. I am tired of my life. What can I do?*

Tears streamed down his cheeks. He would not move to wipe them but just let them fall on his makeshift pillow. He groaned internally in emotional pain. Sometime later, as he lay still, sleep overtook him.

***

Keyloi felt a shake on his shoulder.

"Hey, Keyloi. Time to wake up."

Keyloi jumped. "What time is it?"

"Capria is just now rising, and I have good news. Rescue will be here in four hours."

The vanished feelings of anguish rushed back in. "Wonderful," he responded through sarcasm. He turned his head back to the wall.

After a short pause, Braven asked, "Keyloi, what's wrong? You act as if you don't want to be rescued."

He lay there for a moment and then sat up and leaned against the wall. "It's not that I don't want to be rescued. It's just that I don't have much to look forward to when I return," he confessed.

"What about your parents?"

He dropped his head. "I have no parents."

"Your dad, the physician?"

"He's not my real dad. My parents were killed in a landslide accident at home on Radzier. Dr. Kelba lost his family in the same accident. He was my doctor and wanted to adopt me. Then he was assigned here."

"Did he adopt you?"

"I think so. Maybe. I don't know."

"Oh, Keyloi. If it's not a legal adoption and he's not your legal guardian, that could be kidnapping."

Keyloi looked at the floor. "I don't remember my past, but someone was after me. I needed somewhere safe. He's not safe. He was great at first, but he started…" Keyloi hesitated. His eyes wandered all over the floor. He was too ashamed to talk about it. "I don't want to live with him anymore." He couldn't stop a tear from falling.

"That's a lot for a twelve-year-old to handle. When we return, I'll see what I can do for you. We'll work out something. How about that?"

Keyloi looked at Braven. *Would he really do that?* He could see a glimmer of hope. "Will you do that?" His heartbeat began to increase.

"Of course. I don't know what all can be done, but I'll investigate it."

"Thank you! I'll repay you somehow." *Can I really get away from him? Can Braven do something to help?* He wiped away another tear.

"You're welcome, and you can repay me with another dose."

Keyloi quickly grabbed the last dose of dologra and administered it. He wanted to help his Scout friend any way he could. *I wish I could be like him.*

"How did you get to be so brave?" Keyloi asked.

Braven smiled, "I've not always been brave. It's just the way I've learned how to react in situations."

"Will you teach me? You think I could be a Scout when I get older?"

Braven smiled. "I know you can, and I'd be happy to teach you."

Keyloi was thrilled. He was happy to have Braven as a

friend and mentor. He wanted to live near him wherever they went.

"Capria should have risen by now." Braven slowly opened the door and light flooded their room. "Another night down. Hopefully the last."

Keyloi agreed. He wanted off the planet and away from those monsters. They opened the door into the air portal's central room.

"The caprodomes didn't come here last night," Keyloi observed.

"Yeah, their informant couldn't go to report where we were hiding." They chuckled. "Speaking of the limya," Braven stated, "we need to let it out. We should not be cruel and allow it to starve to death."

Braven went to open the door. As soon as it was opened, the limya ran out and loudly squealed at them both. The sound was not the pleasing squeak they had heard earlier. It ran to the exterior door, returned to them making the same harsh noise, and then back to the exterior door.

"I think it's angry at us." Braven chuckled. "Open the door so it can leave."

Keyloi opened the door, the limya shot outside toward the colony as fast as it could making that obnoxious noise as it sped away.

Braven and Keyloi stood in awe.

"What was that all about?" Keyloi asked.

Braven looked in amazement. "That was strange." He shook his head as a negative reply. "Well," he said, "We have four hours before the rescue is planned. And it will be just outside to the north. Until then, we need to wait."

"Four long hours." Keyloi was stressed. He didn't want to wait another minute.

"Yep. Four long, boring hours. Nothing to do. No one to visit. No caprodomes to torment us. What can happen in four hours? Maybe we should just take a nap," Braven gave a slight smirk.

Keyloi snapped his head toward his senior. "I'm not taking a nap this time. I'm ready to leave."

Both laughed aloud.

Section 22

Keyloi gazed across the landscape. The short vegetation did nothing to pique his interest. He longed to see flora and fauna again like on Radzier. Maybe he could return now. *But who would I live with? I'm all alone.* The lad's excitement dropped.

"I don't think I'll miss this blue planet," Braven's word shook Keyloi from his speculating. They commented about the surroundings and their time at Alpha. Keyloi said he had been on the planet for almost one year. Braven said he had been there sixteen years. *That's longer than I've been alive.*

Keyloi's stomach growled.

"Breakfast?" Braven suggested.

They returned inside for some nourishment. Braven checked the databoard for messages.

"What do you want to do for three hours?"

Keyloi looked at him in dismay. "Stay right here." He thought there was nothing better to do.

Braven chuckled.

About an hour later, they felt a movement.

Keyloi's eyes widened. "Groundquake?"

"Yes." Braven looked concerned. His eyes scanned outside the windows. Keyloi moved closer to the doors. Then he turned and was about to speak but heard something outside. They moved to the next window for a better look, thinking they heard the limya. They both looked through the large, scenic windows. There, bouncing on all fours at the base of the portal structure, was the limya.

"The limya is back," Keyloi said in surprise.

"You're joking. It doesn't take hints very well."

They watched it bounce in one place then to the left and did the same around the building.

"Is it trying to get our attention?" Keyloi wondered aloud.

Braven opened the door and went outside. He walked out onto the veranda and watched the limya do its bouncing act. Keyloi followed him outside.

"What is it doing?" Keyloi asked. "Why is it squealing like it did this morning when we let it out?"

Braven didn't answer but stared at the creature. He walked to where the limya was jumping and stood still as the creature drew closer. It simply arched around him.

"Keyloi, we need to move. Now!"

Braven grabbed his arm and pulled him away from the building. Keyloi joined him in the run, not knowing why they were running. Suddenly, the ground exploded under them.

Keyloi went airborne. He felt a slam to his head and darkness took over.

***

Keyloi found himself facedown. Pain enveloped his head and into his neck. He partially opened his eyes to see thick dust all around him. He couldn't breathe. He coughed. He raised his shirt over his mouth and nose to filter the air.

He heard his name being called in the distance but couldn't breathe well enough to answer. His head swirled in confusion as to what happened. He coughed stronger. Dust invaded his lungs. The coughing caused the pain to increase. He groaned aloud.

Again, he heard his name. "Here." Keyloi gagged and coughed. He heard Braven scream out in pain. *He needs help. I'll be right there.* He coughed and held his head.

"Where are you?" came the voice.

"Here," he coughed. He tried raising up to his knees. He closed his eyes and slowly shook his head.

Braven came into sight. His outer shirt was wrapped around his leg and soaked in blood.

"Keyloi."

"I'm … here. Are you okay?" His words slurred.

"Are you injured?" Braven ignored Keyloi's question.

"My head hurts. I think it's bleeding. And my hand," Keyloi groaned.

"Let's get away from here."

Braven cleared the debris so Keyloi could stand. The youth felt blood streaming down his right cheek. He held his left hand under his right armpit. Braven examined the back of his head.

"The blood's coming from a gash behind your ear." He mentioned that his hand could possibly be broken. He told him to hold his shirt over the cut to help stop the bleeding.

The two helped each other and slowly moved away from the scene of destruction. Braven said the rescue would be north of the air portal, so they headed that direction.

They moved farther away and stopped. Braven wanted to look at everything. The once-useful building was gone, and a huge monolith stood in its place. It was only three meters tall but twice the size of the other monoliths in circumference.

"How did you know when to run?" Keyloi coughed his words.

The Scout paused. "Something didn't seem right." He took in a breath and coughed. "The limya was acting differently. We needed to get away from it."

The limya? Keyloi wondered why he mentioned that creature when a groundquake happened. "What does a limya have to do with a monolith?"

"The limya worked with the caprodomes. Remember the night it ran away from us? It returned and made the coaxing squeak to get us out of our shelter while the caprodomes were waiting for us. The caprodomes work with the monoliths to bring them food. So, I now figure all three creatures work together for survival."

"Oh, I see." Keyloi was in thought. "So, when the limya came back and started dancing around and squealing loudly, it was alerting the monolith?"

"It must be a symbiotic relationship between the three."

Keyloi pondered that triangular connection. "How strange."

"I've never seen or heard of three creatures work together like that. Keyloi, we're on a different planet full of unusual creations. We can't rule out anything, no matter how bizarre."

The limya came around the corner of the debris and stared at them. Its unbearably piercing squeal returned. It ran around the pair and began its dance once again.

"Oh, no you don't." Braven picked up a piece of debris and threw it at the little creature. Keyloi joined in the barrage. The limya ran a few meters toward the monolith still squealing and turned back to view them.

"We need to get away from that thing. Who knows what it will do?" Braven said.

Wherever they moved, the critter was right behind them making its absurd squealing noise.

"Can we lock that thing inside somewhere so it will leave us alone?" Keyloi asked.

"It's not going to let us get close enough to catch it." Braven threw something else at it.

Keyloi threw a piece of debris at it, and it hit the animal in the rump. The limya yipped and ran toward the colony, squealing as it went. The two watched the creature disappear among the buildings.

"You took care of that. Good throw," Braven complimented.

Keyloi was proud of his accomplishment. He watched the exiting creature. *You just try and come back.*

Keyloi bowed his head and touched the side of his face. "My head hurts."

Braven looked at his head injury. He said the bleeding had slowed. He examined his hand which had begun swelling.

"Let's go find a place to rest until they arrive," Braven suggested.

They found some small flat rocks about fifty meters north of the air portal to rest on and wait for their rescue. Neither of them wanted to return to the colony or see any of the creatures again.

Braven removed the blood-soaked shirt to check his leg. Keyloi thought it looked bad. Blood was steadily oozing. He helped him retighten the bandage.

They waited for a long time. Braven said he left the databoard inside the building, so they couldn't contact the rescue teams. They could only guess when help would arrive.

Braven groaned at times, and Keyloi could see his leg and ribs were causing him lots of discomfort. He was glad that he was able to give the Scout the dologra before the explosion.

Keyloi tried to make small talk. "I wonder if everyone is

still at the portal or if they already left to other planets."

"I'm sure they have already started their reassignments. That's part of evacuation and relocation plans. If they remained on the space portal for very long, they would quickly run out of supplies."

Keyloi was amazed at how practical Braven was. He knew so much and always had an answer.

Braven looked up toward the colony. The limya returned toward them at full speed. "Oh, no."

Keyloi followed his eyes to see the approaching critter. "What now?" He picked up a fist-sized rock and readied it.

The squealing started and grew, but this time, it echoed from the colony. Keyloi saw a small group of the creatures following. Five or six limyas were running toward them making the same noise.

They both stood, not knowing what to do. Keyloi knew Braven could not outrun them with his injuries. Braven pulled out his stun pistol. Keyloi grabbed rocks. They were ready for an attack.

The limyas surrounded them and multiplied their ear-piercing squeals and dances. They all bounced in unison.

Keyloi threw rocks. Braven grabbed the few rocks near him and hurled them at the attackers. As the two moved in one direction, the beasts followed them. They all remained in circumference and perfect uniform as if they knew what the other would do.

"We need to get away from these things. Just start heading that way." Braven pointed as he yelled his orders. "They are alerting the monolith of our location."

The two moved to the north, and the limyas moved along with them. They shifted east, and the creatures followed.

They found more rocks and quickly flung them toward their assailants. Braven ignited his pistol toward them, but the flare only leapt twenty-five centimeters. They continued moving back and forth to stay away from a possible monolith explosion.

The creatures would not stop their harassment. Braven and Keyloi felt a small groundquake and quickly made their way farther north. It stopped. The incessant shrieking reverberated through their heads. Keyloi's head was pounding. He wanted to stop and hold it but continued up his barrage.

They continued moving in random ways and did not stop. Keyloi knew Braven was in as much pain as he was, but they had to continue through the agony.

The limyas continued their madness. The humanoids continued their defense.

Wind and dust blew over the scene. Keyloi's fear ignited. The limyas grew louder. He screamed.

The limyas started falling. The defendants made good shots. One after another as if they were being hit by something. A groundquake stirred. Something grabbed Keyloi. He screamed. The pain in his head exploded. The ground erupted. He knew he was about to die. Something picked up Keyloi from behind. He struggled but pain hindered him. He screamed and fought. Fear overtook him.

Section 23

"Be still, boy. You're going to be safe," a voice yelled in his right ear. Keyloi was carried to a hilo and put inside. He quickly found a seat and looked back at the scene. One of the males was carrying Braven.

Braven found a seat, and they went airborne. The last armed member was holding on the side of the hilo, spraying the ground with his weapon for a final blow. Keyloi saw four military personnel. He looked around Braven at the ground to see a new monolith surrounded by clouds of dust and a few limyas still running about.

"Scout Triton?" one of the personnel asked loudly.

"Yes, ma'am, and this is Keyloi Gravton. Thank you for coming."

"Of course, our pleasure," the young female said with a grin.

The hilo flew a few kilometers away to a waiting air shuttle. It landed, and the passengers exited. As they entered the air shuttle, the aircraft collapsed and was loaded into the shuttle.

"Max!" Keyloi said. He had never seen such a vessel.

As they neared the space station, Keyloi was unsure about his future. What would happen to him? Would he have to stay with Dr. Kelba again? Would Braven keep his promise to help him? What could Braven do, anyway? Keyloi didn't even want to see the doctor anymore. His mind swirled with anxiety.

After docking at the space portal, Braven was given an assistance chair because his leg hindered his mobility. Keyloi said he would walk beside his friend. They left the shuttle and made their way to the reception center.

Everyone was in the center to welcome Braven. His parents, friends, and a large group of Scouts. A few welcomed Keyloi, but he didn't know any of them. No one was there to greet him. No one was there. No one cared. Not even the doctor. He watched Braven's reunion for a moment then lowered his head. His heart hurt.

He felt a grasp on his arm and raised his head. "You stay with me. I'm glad we found each other. You helped us to survive. Keyloi, you are my hero." Braven's words grabbed Keyloi's emotions. He slightly smiled. He wiped his eye.

The two were taken to the medical unit for assessment. Braven had three broken ribs and a deep laceration and puncture in his thigh which barely missed his femoral artery. Keyloi had a moderate to severe concussion, two broken fingers, and numerous cuts.

They were given adjoining rooms and kept the door open

all the time. A few times, when someone visited, Braven would ask Keyloi if he could close the door. Of course, Keyloi agreed but felt isolated. Only the attendant visited him. Dr. Kelba didn't even visit. Keyloi didn't like the door closed for very long.

One day, Braven's commander came to see him when Keyloi was in Braven's room. Braven asked the youth if he would let them talk for a few minutes. As usual, Keyloi exited and closed the door. He went to the porthole in his room. The dark spacescape was incredible with its blackness sprayed by the numerous lights that speckled the vastness. His future was bleak. Braven hadn't said anything about his situation, and he would be released from the hospital soon. What was he going to do?

The door opened. The commander came in and asked if he could speak with him.

Why does he want to talk with me? Did they discover who I am? Did they find Dr. Kelba? Keyloi gave a positive answer.

"Scout Triton, or Braven, has informed me of your situation. We have done an investigation and discovered that Dr. Gravton is not your adoptive father nor even your legal guardian," the commander started.

Keyloi's jaw dropped. "But he said he adopted me."

"Evidently, he did not. There are no records of adoption, and we checked the Radzierian hospital where he practiced and Child Protection Departments. Also, there is a long-term warrant on Radzier for him under a different name. Tell me how you and the doctor met."

Keyloi thought for a moment and explained how Dr. Kelba was his doctor, someone was searching for him, he went to the doctor for help, and he took him to his house. Dr. Kelba said he adopted him, and they moved to Jedira.

The commander asked about his personal care with Dr. Gravton. Keyloi looked at the floor. He was ashamed of what the doctor did to him and the anguish he created for him. He answered, "It was fine." His voice barely let out the words.

"We want you and Scout Triton to meet with Dr. Malana Canbossa. She wants to help you cope with some serious experiences you both have encountered. Don't be afraid of her. She is there to help you."

"Okay," he answered quietly.

"In the meantime, we have found a very good temporary place for you to stay until permanent arrangements are made. If it is okay with you, Braven has asked for you to stay with him."

Keyloi brightened. He didn't know how to respond. Tears flooded his eyes. He was overjoyed with this change. He held his breath in excitement. "Uh … yes. It is," he blurted out.

"Good, we will let you stay here with him until he is released, and we will have a place for you both."

"Thank you!"

"I thought you would like that. You can go see him if you wish."

"Thank you." Keyloi ran through the door into Braven's room. Keyloi stared for a moment. Tears streamed down his cheeks.

Braven smiled. "I told you I would take care of you," he said.

Keyloi ran to the bed and hugged his friend. "Thank you," his voice quivered. Nothing else mattered. He was having a victory moment. He knew a change for good was coming.

Braven hugged him back as long as the youth needed comfort.

They were treated and released to their own cabin over the next few days.

Section 24

A week had passed. Braven talked with Keyloi. Braven told him that he had investigated his situation.

"We found information about your family. They were Dr. Relacin and Motatia Kontes, and you had a younger sister named Contia. Your real name is Keyloi Kontes. They were all tragically killed during the Radzierian landslide. It seems Dr. Kelba's family was not killed in the tragedy. He had a wife, and a son named Andaro, who is now around your age."

Shock and anger arose in Keyloi. "He's the one who suggested that name."

"Reports show that he had molested their son, so the mother took the boy, and they fled to another planet. Dr. Gravton changed his identity to Dr. Alam Kelba. When he discovered the authorities were about to arrest him, he disappeared. Now, since you two ended up on Jedira, he has been exposed. Once I reported the information you gave about him to my commander, the former doctor was arrested immediately. He had been wanted by many Radzierian authorities for numerous crimes including fraud, evasion, human trafficking, and ..." Braven hesitated, "child molestation."

Keyloi averted his eyes. *How could I get caught up with such a terrible humanoid? Why didn't I tell someone earlier?* Keyloi hated the doctor for all he had done.

Braven waited a moment. "Keyloi, you won't ever have to see that man again. Once the authorities get finished with him, he will probably be imprisoned at Rejaba."

"He deserves to go there," the young male mumbled.

"And Keyloi, I spoke with my parents about your situation. We all would like you to be a part of our family."

Keyloi looked at Braven. A look of surprise enveloped his features. He tried to speak but only a tear found its way out of him.

"Now, there's a process for us to go through …" Braven was interrupted by the boy.

"You mean to adopt me?" Keyloi was overjoyed.

"The base commander said you can stay with my parents or me until it's completed. Of course, that's if you want to be my little brother." A slight smirk came over Braven's face.

Keyloi quickly made his way to Braven and wrapped his arms around his hero. An unquenchable relief as he had never experienced saturated him. Tears flowed and the only words he could find were a quivery, "Thank you."

"Braven?" a voice came from the doorway.

"Mom, Dad, come on in," he answered as his parents entered.

Keyloi stared at the two entering the room.

"We asked Braven to discuss an adoption with you before we arrived," Dad explained.

"We would be honored for you to call us Mom and Dad." Braven's mother held out her arms to join in the anticipated hugs.

Keyloi quickly approached her for their embrace. Dad put his hand on the lad's shoulder. Keyloi just repeated his appreciation. He would become Keyloi Triton, part of the Triton family, and brother to the man he most admired.

***

The Triton family were all stationed on Eden temporarily until other assignments were created. Braven was also assigned on that planet for further education and work at the Academy.

Keyloi had weekly counseling sessions with Dr. Cambossa about trauma and emotions. Through discussions with her, he discovered that abuse was never acceptable in a family or any type of relationship. Minors were legally protected on all planets from abusive actions. His counselor helped him to overcome and heal from his emotional wounds.

He also attended weekly medical counseling to fully remember his past. He gained memories of his parents, young sister, other family members, Tani Lei, and his best friend, Sabao. He also realized why he could maneuver hustaka moves so easily.

As memories returned, they brought emotional pain. He dwelt on his parents and younger sister. Sabao. Tani Lei. His hustaka coach and entire team. His friends and teachers at school. His grandparents, uncles, aunts, and cousins. His home. His school. The hospital. The walking trails through the forest where he walked every day. He cried. She said it was okay to cry and provided tissues.

During one session, he was taken to a gymnasium with hustaka equipment and pads. Keyloi jumped and grabbed the loops. He tried some of his routines, but he couldn't do his best. He thought of Sabao and their team. He dropped to the floor and on his knees. Emotions erupted. He cried, seemingly, for hours. He lay on his stomach, rolled on his back, sat upright, stood, stomped, jumped, and kicked against the wall mat. He screamed. The loss within him hurt so deeply. Everything he had known as a child was gone. He agonized in mental and emotional pain.

Time passed. He was exhausted and rested on his back. He had no tears left in his body. His mind dulled. He was tired and closed his eyes.

***

He opened his eyes. He looked at the ceiling of the gymnasium. He saw Dr. Cambossa sitting in the corner caringly watching him. She rose and joined him on the floor.

"How do you feel?" she asked quietly.

"I don't know," he answered without emotion.

"It's going to be okay someday. You need emotional healing from the enormous loss you have experienced. It is perfectly healthy to cry and even be angry."

"I am angry. Why did this happen? Now, I'm all alone."

"You are alone from those you knew, but there are worlds of humanoids and some, maybe many, who will be your friends someday, if you will allow them to be."

Keyloi did not respond. Sorrow from grief overwhelmed him.

"This is a transition period for you. Let me help you transition to a new chapter in your book," her kind voice suggested. "I see that you are being adopted by the Triton family. How do you feel about that?"

Keyloi thought of Braven and his parents. "Yes, I like them, and they want me to be their youngest son."

"They are a very good family and have a great reputation in the Alliance. I know they will take good care of you. And their son, Braven, is an outstanding young humanoid who survived numerous life-threatening encounters at his young age. His reputation precedes him. You couldn't ask for a better family to join."

Keyloi was encouraged. He liked them and wasn't surprised about their good character.

***

One week later, a letter of adoption was dispatched to the Triton's concerning Keyloi. It briefly stated that Keyloi Kontes had been officially adopted by Dr. Xaviar Triton and Dr. Trolina Triton as legal guardians and adoptive parents along with all his possessions and responsibilities. The Tritons read the letter to

Braven and Keyloi.

The new family cheered. Keyloi was thrilled to finally have a family he could love. He was thrilled to have Braven as his older brother.

"What does the 'possessions and responsibilities' mean?" Braven asked.

Keyloi was puzzled. He didn't know of any possessions or responsibilities. He was only twelve years old. He shook his head.

"It's probably just regular wording that all letters have," Dad stated.

"What were your parents trades?" Mom asked.

"Uh, my dad was a doctor, kind of a big somebody at the Busonia hospital. My mom was a Level 12 instructor. Why?"

Mom got up and walked slowly around the room. Keyloi looked at her. "Is she okay?" he whispered.

"She's in deep thought. She'll be back in a few minutes," Braven explained.

"Did they leave any inheritance to you?" Dad asked.

"I don't know."

"Do you remember anything from your past at Radzier?" Dad questioned.

"Just that I grew up there, Dad was a doctor, and Mom was an instructor. I was involved in hustaka, but I don't remember much else. I remember my best friend, Sabao. I was older than him by three weeks, but he always said he was older in the brain than me," he chuckled.

"Kontes." Mom interrupted. "Like Dr. Relacin Kontes from Radzier?"

"Yes."

"It makes sense. Dr. Kontes invented the Ossein Cylinder."

Dad turned to Keyloi and asked, "Your father invented the Cylinder?"

Braven and Keyloi just looked at the two adults.

Mom explained to Braven. "The Ossein Cylinder was what healed your skeletal structure and concussion years ago at Delta Colony and now here. It is an invaluable piece of medical equipment."

Dad chimed in, "And if your father owned the patent to it, Keyloi, you're a wealthy person."

Keyloi was speechless.

"Did Dr. Kelba know you had an inheritance?" Dad inquired.

"Not that I know of."

"Did you ever visit with anyone like an attorney?"

"No."

"Did you ever sign anything on his databoard?"

"No."

Dad sat back in his chair. He retrieved his databoard and began to do a search. "I'm going to check on this, and we'll see."

"You mean, I have famols?" Keyloi was surprised.

"Some…what?" Braven asked.

"Uh, credits. Famols is money on Radzier."

"Well, whatever he finds, you're still our son, and we love you whether you're rich or poor." Mom smiled.

***

Another week later, Dad gathered everyone in their central room. "We found out about Keyloi's father. Before the accident, he was the wealthiest humanoid on Radzier, the chairperson of numerous boards, and CEO of Radzier's Medical Professionals Board. He owned the rights to fourteen different patents for medical equipment, which are actively used on every planet in the multiverse today. He owned several properties and businesses on Radzier. After his death and Keyloi's disappearance, trust of the companies under his name maintained the majority of the funds but used a percentage for research and development. There is an administrator that oversees the company's projects."

The three looked at Keyloi.

"What does that mean?" Confusion crossed Keyloi's face.

"Dear son," Mom exaggerated her feelings, "it means you are wealthy."

Keyloi's expression showed his surprise. "You mean Dr. Kelba didn't take it?"

Everyone laughed.

"Let me do some more research and contact a few people at Radzier to see what this is all about and what it means for you," Dad explained.

"Can you contact someone I know on Radzier? I'd like to see her again."

"I'll try. What is her name?"

"Nurse Dala. Uh, I don't know her last name," Keyloi thought. "She was a nurse at the hospital where I was."

"I'll see what I can do."

***

Days later, Dad once again gathered the family and informed them that he had contacted officials from Radzier who were ecstatic that the missing Kontes heir had finally been located and was still alive. He also notified the estate who put him in contact with Nurse Dala. She was overjoyed at the thought that Keyloi still lived and made plans to visit him when he came.

Arrangements were made for Keyloi to visit his home planet of Radzier. Dr. Triton joined him on the journey.

Keyloi received a huge reception with many humanoids attending. All of whom he did not know. The director of his accounts gave them a tour of his assets and properties. He was overwhelmed by everything that he now owned.

The administrator explained, "Everything has been maintained under the last will of your father as closely as possible. Since you had disappeared, after five years, the estate was to be sold and disbursed to any living heir. We are very happy to welcome your return."

Keyloi didn't know what to say but thanked him.

"Keyloi wanted me to ask a few questions," Dr. Triton

stated. "Now that he has returned as the owner of the property, he won't be living on Radzier, but with us, his new family, currently at Eden. How will this affect his possessions?"

"We can secure an attorney who will create whatever Keyloi's wishes would be. He will need an official administrator of the heirship and one to manage all affairs," the adult clarified.

"Can I get famols wherever I am?" Keyloi piped in.

"Of course. We can transfer any amount to you at any time and as often as you wish. Depending on the distance, it may take a few hours or days."

"Can I get some for my new parents?" Keyloi looked at his new father. Dr. Triton gave him a frown and shook his head.

"Of course. They are your famols, and you can do whatever you wish to do with it.

"Max. Also, can I give some to Tani Dala? Like as much as she needs?"

"Whatever you wish to do. We shall discuss this with your attorney. We will set it up however you wish. Just understand that because of your age, there will be a counselor assigned to guide you in all decisions," he explained.

After the quick business meeting, he and Dr. Triton went to spend time with Nurse Dala. Dad enjoyed meeting his son's old friend and experiencing life on Radzier.

They visited Nurse Dala often who always had scotia ready for him. He endowed enough famols to her that she would have all she wanted for the rest of her life.

After all the affairs were settled, Keyloi said goodbye to his companions, and he joined his new father on the long journey back to his new family on Eden.

Check out the other books in The Journeys of Braven Series and this author.

The Jediran Quest, Book 1

The Mines of Jedira, Book 2

The Secrets of Jedira, Book 3

ABOUT THE AUTHOR

Cal Davis created and wrote stories when he was a teenager. He just didn't like reading at school, because there was always an exam. Reading should be for fun, right? After college (and a lot of reading!), he enjoyed a couple of overseas tours in the Air Force and ended up teaching middle school. A few years later, he took a position in the housing industry, working on 30-years for retirement.

Cal loves writing and telling stories with purpose for children. He wrote the picture books "I'm Just a Crow" and "Look, Look, Look What I Did!" to show children to be the person they were created to be and not cave to peer pressure. His award-winning books, "The Jediran Quest" and "The Mines of Jedira," of the *Journeys of Braven Series* gives examples of leadership and character-building for young teens. Many of his books grant Accelerated Reading (AR) points for primary and middle schoolers. He enjoys helping other authors in their pursuit of the literary world and still believes *Reading should be fun!*

Email: caldavisauthor@gmail.com

Website: www.caldavisauthor.com

Facebook: www.facebook.com/caldavisauthor

www.ingramcontent.com/pod-product-compliance
Lightning Source LLC
Chambersburg PA
CBHW051954220626
47052CB00004B/946